Through the bars Julia could see Billy's back moving as he pried at the board. The groaning sound as wood separated from wood echoed in her head.

As she lifted herself off her knees, she noticed the key protruding from the iron box on the gate of the grille. Stupid Billy, he had locked himself in again.

She was about to call to him. If she pointed it out, he would come away from his work and they would laugh together over the mistake.

Then Julia remembered that they didn't laugh over things together anymore . . .

THE CAGE

Susan Cheever

FAWCETT CREST • NEW YORK

For my parents
John and Mary Cheever

The sickness of the family is the fear of risk. Its credo is the economy of self.

—*Anonymous*

Chapter 1

HE WAS ALREADY LATE. As he stepped on the down escalator, William Bristol watched the ornate hands of the clock on the information booth click past another minute. Below him the vaulted waiting room of Grand Central echoed with the watery roar of a thousand human voices and the guttural rumble of departing rush-hour trains. On the ceiling, Orion raised his club toward Lexington Avenue in a constellation of light-bulb stars. A few faces in the crowd turned to watch the tall man's descent as they passed him moving upward on the opposite escalator. He pushed his sand-colored hair off his high forehead, and looked quickly at his gold wrist watch. Six thirty-nine; he had made her wait for him again.

Bristol inventoried his excuses. Traffic at the construction sites on Madison, a telephone call from the coast, an unexpected story conference with Walter Sachs, a slow watch. Throwing himself forward toward Track 30, he brushed against a long-haired girl leaning down to unload a huge blue backpack, sidestepped the ulcerated legs of a wino who slumped against the wall, and just missed colliding with a fat woman in a beige suit who had stopped in the middle of the floor to consult her guidebook, causing a slight swell of the human tide on either side of her as the mass of commuters hurried through the station toward home.

His wife was waiting with her back turned, looking toward the arcade of bagel shops and greasy spoons behind Track 38, where they used to roll a red carpet out onto the marble floor when the Twentieth Century Limited came in from Chicago. She still had the pale hair and confident shoulders of a beauty, a sparkling American girl from the 1950s when everyone drank martinis, and all the wives were pregnant, and the people you knew from the beach in the summer were your neighbors back in the suburbs or in the big old apartments on the Upper East Side. He thought of rolling lawns where beech trees throw shadows on summer afternoons, and firelit parlors in New England with the Christmas snow piled high outside, and country villages where the tradesmen know everybody's name. From behind, Julia's body showed no signs of the passage of time: the disappointments of middle age, the erosions of rearing a child, the agony of marriage to a man who was always late.

"Oh there you are, Billy." She turned toward him. "I was late, I'm glad you didn't have to wait for me."

He panted to a stop and felt the rest of the crowd go rushing on without him. It was going to be all right this time. As he bowed to kiss her cool cheek he felt the sweat and grit of the city settle over him like a second skin. "Was it hot driving in? I booked a table at the Algonquin," he said.

"I had to wait in line to get into the garage. The Algonquin?"

"Would you rather somewhere else?"

"No, that sounds fine." Her voice suggested that whatever he had chosen was perhaps not quite exactly what she would have chosen. "You'd think that with the prices that garage charges there wouldn't be a line."

He guided her firmly up the stairs and through the glass doors. As they stepped out onto Vanderbilt Avenue the unseasonable heat was like a shove to the chest, knocking him back a step and filling his throat with the smell of asphalt and automobile exhaust. It was a record for May. The predictable weather story had been clacking out over the AP wire as he walked through the newsroom on his way out. The heat meant that his tie was strangling him, his shirt rubbed angrily against wet flesh, his swollen feet jammed against the implacable ends of his tasseled loafers. If it weren't for their Thursday-night dinners in the city, he would be on the train now, half an hour away from a real drink, a cool shower, and loose, fresh clothes.

They crossed Forty-third Street in front of the Biltmore, and Bristol's eyes swiveled toward a pair of shoulders getting out of a taxicab in front of the revolving doors to the hotel. One long leg emerged below them, exposed by a slit skirt that fell away above the knee. He concentrated on expanding his peripheral vision without attracting Julia's attention by moving his head. Flash: long blonde hair. Flash: a minute white halter over tanned flesh. Flash: high heels as she slammed the taxi door and walked through the doors and out of his visual reach.

Julia walked confidently beside him, looking out at the world from the shelter of his nearness, her marriedness. When they were together she still had the self-assured sparkle that had brought suitors from as far away as Princeton and even Stanford when she was a co-ed. Charley North's only daughter Julia, and everyone knew that the old man had money. Her hair was the color of champagne, and her skin as pale as winter air, with a translucent tracery of vein showing through at her forehead and throat. Julia North was the kind of girl Bristol knew he wanted but thought he never could have. So completely had she expected him to love her and to marry her that it almost left him no choice. There were summers at Northwood, and winter vacations at ski resorts, and the covetous, congratulatory looks on other men's faces when they saw him with her.

But sometimes when he saw her alone, waiting for him at Grand Central, or driving away from the Ash Hill station as his train pulled out, or standing at the end of an aisle in the supermarket, she seemed so lost and isolated that he wanted to look away. He was glad she hadn't had to wait alone for him this time.

Drivers honked and inched forward, and idling buses hiccupped oily fumes in the traffic jam at the corner of Fifth Avenue. Blasts of heat hit the simmering pavement as they passed each building. He put an arm around her shoulders, guiding her across in front of two stopped cars and behind the crumpled fender of a black delivery van.

"You look terrific," he said. "Very summery."

She tilted her face up, crinkling the skin around her eyes into a smile. A slight reluctance in her gaze reminded him that his sweaty hand was probably staining the airy fabric of her blouse. He let his arm drop and she took it by the elbow. A new pool of sweat formed under his sleeve in the hollow of his crooked arm.

The hotel lobby was dark and cool after the harsh brightness outdoors, and the dimness blinded him as they passed the registration desk and walked through the bar.

"Look over there, in that armchair," Julia whispered emphatically, pulling his elbow with one hand and gesturing vaguely into the darkness with the other. He peered into the corner of the room, trying to speed up the adjustment of his vision to the low light. A group of people sat around a table under a parchment wall sconce; he still couldn't see their faces.

"Isn't that someone we know?" Her hand tightened on his arm. Again he strained his eyes, and again a muddle of featureless drinkers was all the effort yielded.

"Could be," he said, shrugging. Preoccupation and the heat dulled his senses, and he turned to the figure of the headwaiter in the doorway of the dining room.

"I sort of hope not." Julia relaxed her hold and followed him through the door with a giggle. "Did you see that *girl* he was with? She looked about fifteen. It might have been embarrassing." The headwaiter moved the table out for Julia's passage, and she relaxed against the banquette with the assurance of a woman who was the right age, wearing the right clothes, having the right kind of evening with the right kind of man.

The Algonquin Hotel is situated in the middle of Manhattan Island, just a block away from the Harvard Club, the offices of *The New Yorker* magazine, and the sleazy topless bars and porno theaters on the east side of Broadway. Because of its proximity to some of these landmarks, it has always been a literary gathering place of raffish sorts. This is where Dorothy Parker and Robert Benchley decided to call their efforts Parkbench, this is where George S. Kaufman sharpened his wits on Alexander Woollcott, this is where Harold Ross used to bring young writers to yell at them over lunch, and this is where *The New Yorker*'s current editor has his invariable noontime order of a glass of milk and dry white toast served in a silver rack.

The big bar looks like a club for Victorian gents, with chairs and velvet sofas pushed together against wooden paneling. But instead it is usually crowded with garment-district traders looking for a respite from the coffee shops on Seventh Avenue, tourists who have read about New York's most accessible literary mecca in their Fodor's or Mobil Guide, and suburban couples like the Bristols who go there because it's so convenient and because it has changed so little over the years.

The bar was crowded at this hour, but the dining room was empty. It was just seven o'clock on a Thursday evening at the end of May, and two waiters standing idly at the far end of the room near the kitchen were the only other inhabitants of the long paneled space. Julia's weekly dinners in town were always early, because she didn't like to drive after dark. And Bristol liked to get home before eleven for a full night's sleep before he turned around and got in the car to drive to the train to come into the city again in the morning. He felt like a human yo-yo. Not for them the glamour and glitter of the New Yorkers who crowded chic restaurants at eight-thirty, or at ten-thirty after the theater. In a few hours those people would fill this very room that was now strangely abandoned and empty. Chatter and laughter would carom off the rich wooden walls, lovely women in evening dresses would lift glasses of champagne, the two lackadaisical waiters would snap attentively from table to table, taking orders for caviar, and smoked salmon, and exotic brandy concoctions. By then the Bristols would be gone, leaving no traces behind on the red leather of their banquette. As people at this table relaxed and smiled at each other and discussed the latest Broadway hit, Bristol would be wearily guiding the station wagon into the two-car garage at Ash Hill.

He wrapped his sweating hand around the slim stem of the martini glass. Cold gin coated the sides of the glass with a velvety transparence, keeping a prim lemon peel afloat. Bristol concentrated on the stinging, metallic taste of juniper as the liquor slid down his dry, hot throat with its certain, inevitable effect. Another swallow; he could almost feel his temperature drop. The drink hit his brain with a loving nudge, and he leaned back against the wall.

"That feels good," he said.

"Poor Billy, did you have a hard day?" Julia sipped a glass of white wine.

"Not really, it's just hot." Another swallow. There was no point in bringing back the torrid, Byzantine intricacies of the magazine just as they were beginning to recede in his mind. The computer had gone down again, the files for the alcoholism cover story he was working on were coming in too slowly, pictures for the rodeo story were missing, and one of the other writers was sick and he had had to pound out a sidebar on bathing-suit couture at the last minute; and even so Barry had made a fuss about his leaving early. Just another day in the life of a prize-winning magazine writer. When the waiter brought their dinners, he ordered another martini.

"There was a letter from Cece today," Julia said. "Could I have a glass of Perrier with this?"

"Any news?" The sausage in Bristol's plate of mixed grill made a neat crescent around the steak and kidneys. He cut through the meat, releasing a stream of salty juice. If there had been any bad news, he knew she would have told him right away.

"It sounds like she's moving in with Jerry. I wish they would learn not to put so much butter on this sole."

He reached for the fresh martini. "Did she say that?"

"No, but she might as well have. I get the feeling he may be a little bit reluctant about the whole thing." The piece of bacon at the edge of his plate shattered into slivers under the pressure of his fork. Julia could never believe that men were interested in her daughter. He was always convinced that they were interested, and it terrified him. He used his spoon to scoop the bacon into his mouth while Julia's attention was distracted by her salad.

What was it like? Bristol found it hard to understand modern courtship, a process that seemed to begin *after* sex—the same sex that had been the end result of courtship, in his courting days. Cecile had always been intensely curious about her parents' romance, as if their way of going about it had no relation to her own world. The customs of the 1950s seemed antique and delightful to her, as odd and out of place as the shining suits in the Armor rooms that Bristol took her — to see in the Metropolitan Museum, or the tiny canopied beds and child-sized chairs upstairs in the American Wing. *William and Julia—Billy and Julie,* she would say, giggling over the strangeness of names of the two people most familiar to her. *Please tell me more about Billy and Julie.*

Instead of bedtime stories, Bristol would tell her about

homecoming weekends at Brown, rivalries at the Holiday Dances, and crises in the men's room at the River Club. She loved the story about the Harvard-Brown game, and the time that Julia stayed with her Aunt Laura on Waterman Street and Billy climbed through the window to leave flowers in her room and brought the drainpipe and the old lady's wrath down on his head as he exited. Her handsome father had beat out his dreadful rivals: Max, the dashing graduate student with the red MG; Nick, the English professor who wanted to take Mommy to live on the Riviera; Rob Jenkins, the big cozy banker who was now Cecile's honorary Uncle Rob—characters as horrible in their potential evil as Farmer McGregor in Peter Rabbit, or Stewie Stinker in her book about the bandit who robbed the Christmas train. Their courtship was the family mythology, a tale of perilous journeys (the train from New York to Providence), troll-like villains placated (Grandpa Charley North), and fatal mischances narrowly averted (Julia's unmailed) letter accepting Nick: an Ivy League Odyssey with the happiest of all possible endings. Love! Marriage! The birth of a little girl.

After dinner, Bristol and Julia walked across the street to the parking lot, and Bristol paid for the car and slid into the driver's seat as he always did when they drove together. As he turned the car north onto the West Side Highway, his wife rummaged in her pocketbook for a package of cigarettes. Cellophane crackled; she pushed in the automatic lighter on the dashboard.

"I'm going to try and stop next month when I go up to New Hampshire," she said. "Well, I didn't have any before dinner." The elevated highway lifted them over block after block of apartment buildings; he imagined thousands of couples living behind their lighted windows, and thousands of women telling their husbands such harmless lies. Smoke from her cigarette filled his lungs with an unpleasant tickle, and he visualized her mouth puckering around the lipstick-stained filter. The smell of stale tobacco drifted up from her purse, cutting through the buzz of pleasure left over from his dinnertime gin. His head was foggy, but the road was familiar. The air was cooler now, and the strobe effect of the streetlights played across the inside of the station wagon. Ahead of them the George Washington Bridge made a sparkly bracelet across the dark Hudson. The seams in the asphalt roadway beat a soothing rhythm against the tires.

Chapter 2

THE SHRIEK OF THE ALARM CLOCK frightened Julia out of a deep sleep and dreams of a piny New Hampshire lakeshore. She lurched forward to turn it off, bruising her wrist on the bedside table. On the other side of the mattress Billy groaned and rolled over, tangling his pajamas with the edge of the sheet and pulling it free of the bed.

"Oh shit," he said.

"Billy." She let her voice remind him that she hated that word. He stumbled past her and slammed the bathroom door behind him.

In the kitchen, she turned the gas on under the kettle and measured coffee beans into the grinder. As the water heated she pushed two pieces of bread into the toaster and got a carton of eggs out of the refrigerator. A package of cigarettes fell off the rounded top of the refrigerator when she shut the door, and she quickly stuffed it into the china cabinet as footsteps came toward her across the dining room.

"The little car's still at the garage," she said, pouring hot water into the top of the drip pot. "They're fixing the fuel-injection system."

"I'd like to catch the eight forty-five."

"Do you want me to drive you to the station?"

"Would you mind?" He folded a piece of the toast into his mouth and held out his cup for coffee.

"You've got time for some scrambled eggs," she said. Instead of answering her, he stood up and brushed the toast crumbs off the lapels of his tan poplin suit.

"That tie looks nice." It was a blue patterned silk that Cece had sent from San Francisco at Christmas.

"We'd better get cracking," he said. "I don't want to miss the train."

Sometimes she found herself wishing that something would intervene, as she stood there in her slept-in nightgown pouring coffee for this freshly showered man in a good suit and crisp light-blue shirt smelling faintly of Pears soap. A country snowstorm in the winter, or an electrical breakdown on the Harlem Division trains in the summer. The intensity of his desire to get to work seemed like a rebuff. A few times a year he caught cold and stayed home for a day—but even then, his office called him almost every hour. What if he was sick more often? What if he retired and was home all the time, like some men? He would be here to help out and keep her company; and he would see how hard she worked, how much she did for him.

Now she put a raincoat on over her nightgown and followed him out to the garage. When she got back she would do the breakfast dishes and get dressed. Then there was shopping. The flower border in front of the house had to be weeded. She ought to make an appointment with Mrs. Griffon about the upstairs bedroom. The thought of Mrs. Griffon reminded her of work to be done. Dust in the kitchen corners reproached her, egg-tarnish spots on the silver called her names. The station wagon was overdue for its 20,000-mile service. Her head began to ache as she rode past the Kensico Reservoir and down Route 22, chauffeured by her silent, preoccupied husband.

It was afternoon by the time she put the groceries away. Lettuce in the vegetable crisper, eggs in the shallow indentations molded into the refrigerator door, flour in the big blue canister. If she was going to bake a dessert, it would have to be a cake from that mix the cleaning lady had bought once by mistake. That was good enough. Her mother had never baked a cake in her life, Julia thought. There were always servants in the big dark kitchen downstairs where none of them were allowed to go.

Each morning her mother sat down with the cook and planned the menus for the day. Dinner for the grownups. Dinner for little Julie. If she and Charley were entertaining, Julie would eat earlier and be sent upstairs before the guests came. Sometimes she was brought back again, clean and fragrant after her detested bath, to kiss a special friend goodnight. Later she would creep out of bed, footstep by careful footstep, and sit at the top of the stairs listening to the warmth of the grownups' conversation and watching the flickering lights from below.

Nobody lived like that anymore. Her mother's married life had been spent planning meals, arranging flowers, redecorating Northwood and the house on Eighty-first Street, and dealing with the servants. What would the glamorous Cecile North think of her daughter now: doing everything for herself, even dinner parties, with only a doltish girl to come in once a week for the light cleaning. Many of the people she and Billy knew were better-off than their parents had been. Most of them had grown up in other cities, the children of shopkeepers and schoolteachers. Not Julia. Even her mother had been a celebrated beauty, one of the great debutantes. And her father was Charley North, the fabulous elegant Charley North, businessman, entrepreneur, showman, heartbreaker, magician and millionaire.

In the evening when he came home from his office downtown, she would show him the curtsy she had learned at Mrs. Wolf's dancing classes, or the cartwheels they had taught her in rhythm class at Brearley, and he would grab her up in his strong arms and wheel her around the living room, landing her in his lap on the big puffy sofa in front of the fireplace. *You're my little Princess*, he would say, *my little Principessa.* He smelled of bourbon, and good tobacco, and Irish tweed. And when Charley North came back from one of his famous trips, there were always wonderful presents for Julie: dresses edged with Irish lace, ballerina costumes with tutus and toe shoes, watercolor boxes and easels from London, and stuffed animals bigger than she was! Now Julia looked around her ruefully. The small kitchen, the emptied supermarket bags, the congealing remains of her tuna-fish-salad lunch. How had her life become so ordinary?

There was still some money, of course, although it turned out that her father had always acted a lot richer than he really was. The money was locked up in trusts and bonds, most of them in Cece's name, but the interest was enough for them to have a few luxuries that Billy's salary never would have stretched to. This house, a few good antiques, the services of Mrs. Griffon, her mother's decorator, and three-star restaurants when they had gone to France a year ago after Cece left for Berkeley. At least she never had to go out and get a job like some of the women they knew. Nothing looked sillier than a middle-aged woman all dressed up like a career girl with a briefcase and a little gray suit.

And best of all, they still owned Northwood, with its great turreted house and big old barn and rolling pastures down to the lake. These days just keeping the place up and paying the taxes on it was a big drain. Her father was from a time before taxes. Now the roof needed reshingling and the paint was beginning to fade; the flower gardens had gone to seed. Just last spring she had had the big vegetable garden plowed under and planted with grass, leaving herself one fenced-in corner for a tiny patch of tomatoes, lettuce, strawberries and herbs. Darwin Gibbs still planted the garden in early spring and came up from Granville Center once a week during the summer to help out, but she did most of the work herself, and that was on top of opening the big house each spring and cleaning it and trying to find someone from the village to help with the mowing and to scythe the lower pasture. It was worth it, though. Northwood's shabby magnificence and its empty spaces represented a final remnant of her father's kind of life—and the proof of her own continuing specialness.

The afternoon school bus had passed down on Popham Road by the time she got out to the flower bed. The long metal claws of her cultivator scratched open the winter-hardened earth, releasing the rooty smell of underground. The magnolia was out, and the dogwood with petal clusters like ladies' hands in immaculate white gloves waved at the edge of the lawn. Julia carefully turned over the soil around each plant. The tulips were up, and the daffodils and the hyacinths. A few weeks ago they had been juicy green shoots, indistinguishable from each other except in her memory. She put the cultivator down to take off her cardigan as the sun warmed her up. In the city, the heat would be brutal. As she pulled the gray cashmere over her head, the top buttons caught in the hair at the back of her neck. A truck rumbled by on the road at the moment the sweater obscured her vision, and she had a flash of fear and disorientation.

She couldn't see. What if the truck turned up the driveway? Lately the local papers had seemed full of stories about burglaries and worse things. A year ago men had broken into the Hamleys' place at night and raped Sally Hamley before they ransacked the house. Robbers had murdered that whole family over in Pound Ridge. Since Sandy had died at Christmas she didn't even have a watch dog to warn her if someone tried to get in. The old Parker twenty-gauge that her father had used for skeet shooting was still in the attic. Sometimes she took it out of the morocco leather case with his initials on it and ran her hands over the stock and chasings. Her father had taught her to shoot, with the shotgun and with the Remington .22 that was still in the corner of the linen closet up at Northwood. If someone ever did come, she hoped they would arrive when she had that in her hands.

As the truck rumbled off down the hill she relaxed, and her thoughts returned to pansies and petunias. The iris and wisteria would be out before she went up to New Hampshire in June, but by then the tulips and daffodils would be dead. Then there would be the sweet blossoms of the lilac bush—once a knotted skeleton at the corner of the house. Because New Hampshire's climate was colder, she always had two springs. Here, in May and early June, and at Northwood, where everything was a month behind. She tied her sweater around her waist and stooped to work, clearing away the old leaves and redefining the edge of the border.

Progress hypnotized her. She knew it was time to stop, but the end of the border at the far side of the house came seductively closer, calling to her that she might as well finish the job, wooing her with the satisfaction of order, neatness, completion. She thought of Billy hurrying across Grand Central at this moment, on marble floors under the starry ceiling. Her treacherous mind slipped her an image of him kissing another woman good-by for the night at the gate to Track 30. They were standing next to the signboard that announced the departure of the North White Plains Express at 5:22. The woman had her back turned, but she was young and tall with straight long hair like Cece's. The cultivator slipped in Julia's hand, raking across the petals of the daffodils. Billy wouldn't do that, even if everyone else did. He wasn't like Harry Covert or Sam Noble, who had left his wife out here and moved into the city—everyone knew why.

No, Billy would be sweaty and worn out, slouched in his habitual fog in the creaky seat of the Harlem Division coach, wearily producing his monthly pass as the conductor came through. And by the time the express pulled into North White Plains, she would have finished the border and driven down to the station to wait in the line of wives' station wagons that formed at the entrance to the parking lot before the train came in. Just as she always did. Behind her afternoon shadows striped the lawn with darkness where it sloped down to the row of maple trees that separated their property from the road.

Chapter 3

BY JUNE, THE UNSEASONABLE HEAT HAD settled in for the summer. Bristol wiped sweat off his forehead with a linen handkerchief as he stepped through the swinging doors into the high marble lobby of his building. The elevator man nodded as he stepped in and the doors closed, and the upstairs eleventh-floor receptionist smiled as he went by.

"Hot enough for you?" he asked her, heading down the hall as she hummed the standard note of assent. The telephone was ringing as he stepped through the door to his office. He dropped his briefcase on a chair in front of the bookshelves, and knocked over a pile of wire copy and newspaper clips as he reached across his desk for the receiver.

"Could Walter see you when you have a minute?" The editor-in-chief's secretary had a way of asking a question that made it feel like a karate chop.

"I'll be right there." Bristol flipped through the messages in his In box; there might be something he should know about before seeing the boss. Sammy Short invited him to a party for Lauren Long at Disco Heaven, the copy department wanted him to call ASAP, Janet Talent had called twice . . . who the hell was that? And Jack Homes from the Chemical Bank. Oh God, had he bounced another check? The telephone was ringing again as he walked out the door.

"Sherry, can you get that?" His secretary looked up from the newspaper as he passed her desk. She looked even more morose than usual. "I want a light coffee and a cheese Danish, call Janet Talent and find out who she is, I'll be in Walter's office."

"Don't say good morning," she said as he sped past. He could see that he was going to have to add a sulky secretary to his list of things to take care of if he was going to get anything at all done this week.

He straightened his tie as he passed the vacant offices of the two sportswriters, the relentless paper-spewing wire machines, the bank of telephones on the news desk where Angie Pakula was taking two overseas calls at once, the row of clocks in International showing the time in seven different zones. It was 10:00 P.M. in Hong Kong. Both of Walter's secretaries were busy, and Bristol waited, pacing back and forth on the gray industrial carpet in the anteroom of the magazine's main office. Walter liked to summon people to come immediately, and then make them wait. Now his door opened and he stepped forward to put a pile of scrawled memos on his number-one secretary's desk.

"Walter?" Bristol stopped him as he headed out of the anteroom toward the hall. He was a heavy man with massive, ruddy features, an all-star quarterback from the glory days at Harvard who had rushed the front lines of journalism and scored. Bristol reached over to tap the bulging shoulder under Walter's immaculate tailoring. His own hand looked slim and white against the expanse of blue linen.

"Oh, Bill." Walter executed a quarter-turn in his direction without stopping his trajectory toward the door. Something much more important was going on somewhere else. "Did anyone tell you we killed the paperback story? National needs the space." And he was gone.

Bad news again. The paperback story was almost finished, and turning out well. In spite of his editorial rank, Bristol's stories were often dropped at the last minute for the more "important" news; politics and war, a skirmish in a South American country no one had ever heard of, the health of the secretary of state. When a piece he had been assigned to write was killed, Bristol felt a sense of simultaneous relief and dread; relief because he didn't have to do the work, dread because if they didn't need his stories it was only a matter of time until they wouldn't need him, senior editor or no senior editor. He quick-stepped back down the hall to his own office, smiling good morning to Jack Gilson, in Business, and Angie Pakula as he passed. On the clocks in International he saw that it was 10:20 in New York; 10:20 on Monday morning. The week hadn't even begun.

"They've killed the paperback story, are you free for lunch?" He knew she would be. Sherry actually smiled. Having lunch with her wouldn't be any fun, but it was the kind of conciliatory gesture that would buy her good will for a week or two; and the good will of a top secretary was as necessary to Bristol's job as the typewriter, or the clips. When he had been promoted to senior editor last year, Bristol had picked Sherry out of the pool for his personal secretary. Plain girls make the best workers. Because she was lonely, she didn't mind the late nights and long hours. Sometimes she sulked, but Bristol knew that a lunch with the boss was probably the social occasion of the month for her. She would be on the telephone the minute he passed her desk, calling her few friends and getting a lot of half-assed advice about what to demand from him. A raise, an opportunity to do research, more vacation time. Not that she had anywhere to go. Was there ever a time when lunch was less than a confrontation? When it was just a way to provide the body with simple nutrients from the four essential food groups? "She gives good lunch," Jack Gilson had said about one of the business researchers—as if it were sex. The telephone was ringing again as he sprinted the last few steps.

He picked up the receiver, and the lighted button signifying a call on an outside line stopped flashing. Instead, the lighted button that was the direct intercom line to Sherry flashed, and the telephone emitted two nerve-jangling squawks. As he pressed the button connecting him to his secretary, his other outside line began to ring, flashing another button on the panel at the bottom of the telephone.

"Hold a minute, Sherry," he ordered, punching the outside-line button.

"Hear your story got killed. Want to have lunch?" It was Frank Cushing calling from his office at the other end of the hall. Cushing had hired Bristol when he first came to the magazine. Cushing had helped him along. Now Bristol had been given Cushing's job, and the elegant writer, suddenly an old man at sixty-two, had been rusticated to a smaller office with nothing to do. Sometimes they gave him a little story to write, or a minor editing job if the magazine was shorthanded. But Franklin Cushing had been one of the great writers in the early days—and now he was nobody.

"Let me call you back, Frank," Bristol said.

"Right." Bristol hung up by pressing the intercom button; his elbow slipped on the desk, banging the telephone against his In box and sending a new stack of messages flying in the air like square pink confetti.

"Sherry," he said into the receiver. A dull pain spread across his upper back.

"It's your wife," she said.

"Thanks, Sherry." He pressed the other outside-line button and relaxed into his desk chair, lining his aching spine up against the cushioned seat. "Hi, Julie," he said. "What's up?"

"I just wanted to tell you the estate check finally got here so you can pay that American Express bill," she said. "Dom says the little car needs a new carburetor."

"The good news and the bad news." Bristol opened the *Washington Post* at the top of the stack of out-of-town newspapers on his desk.

"Sherry certainly doesn't sound too friendly," Julia said. Bristol flipped through the news pages to the Style section. He could never take his wife's curiosity about his secretary very seriously.

"Does she still have a crush on you?"

The second story in the section was a review of a book on Alcoholics Anonymous. Bristol put the metal edge of his ripstick against the grimy printed page and tore upward. It was a nuisance about the car. "Does Dom think he can get a new carburetor right away?" he asked.

"I guess you don't want to talk about it."

He lifted the square of type off the page and put it in one of the folders on alcoholism that were accumulating on the windowsill behind him. Something in Julia's voice sounded a distant alarm signal in his head. "What's the trouble, sweetie?" he asked.

"Nothing."

He imagined the pale-blue vein in her temple pushing against the white flesh. "Don't be angry." The button for the intercom line to Sherry's desk lit up and the telephone squawked loudly. "Listen Julie, I have to get that, okay? I'll see you later." She hung up before he could say good-by. Sherry appeared in the doorway with a cup of coffee.

"No Danish," she said. "This was the best I could get." Oil oozed against the cellophane of a packaged raisin cake. He picked at the plastic edge of the coffee-cup cover as he walked over to the window. Underneath, the drink was a swirly pale brown.

"Thanks, Sherry." Ten stories below him in the street two workmen were drilling at the concrete sidewalk with jackhammers. Bodies fibrillated as they hung onto the machines, beating to the noise that seemed to shake the earth and the buildings around them. Across Madison Avenue a new building was going up, and all spring Bristol's working day had been punctuated by the shrill sound of the blast-warning whistle and the pounding of dynamite as the foundation was cleared. An office was being remodeled on the floor above him, and the high metallic shriek of an electrical saw filtered through the acoustical tiles on Bristol's ceiling. As he picked up the telephone to placate his guilt with a word to Frank Cushing, another twinge of pain lodged in his lower back.

"It's nothing serious yet," the doctor had said. "You're a good candidate for heart trouble, try to ease off a bit." He had slapped at Bristol's pale, exposed abdomen. "Let me know if you have any other symptoms. Anything at all." After that, Bristol had every symptom he had ever read about. Sharp pain across the left shoulder. Sudden chills. Shortness of breath. Tachycardia so severe it felt as if his heart might burst right out of his skin. He didn't want to bother the doctor.

At noon he guided Sherry across Park Avenue by the elbow. She was a tall, broad-shouldered girl, and he sometimes had the impression that it was difficult for her to get underway without a firm hand against her arm or shoulder.

"You look good today," he said. Bristol prided himself on his ability to get along with secretaries. "It's about time we had lunch together."

"You're usually too busy." Sherry rarely skipped a beat on the job, but her tone often seemed calculated to remind him that she *could* skip a beat. She could make trouble, if he pushed her. At the office party after his promotion, he had put his hands on her broad shoulders and kissed her on the mouth. Instead of sealing their friendship, that kiss seemed to release a resentment and moodiness that he was still paying for. No wonder nobody wanted to work with women.

Sherry primly ordered a salad and a glass of wine. As she picked at a wedge of tomato with her fork he had a vision of her alone in her working-girl's-apartment kitchenette, hunched over a bag of cookies, stuffing a handful into her mouth and groping in the bag with the other hand. He picked up his martini glass and watched the lemon peel work its way up through the machine-made ice cubes. The drink was pale yellow and stinging on the tongue—too much vermouth. He raised the glass toward her and smiled.

"Here's to working together on the alcoholism cover," he said.

"You're going to need me."

"I couldn't do it without you, Sherry." She raised her glass and allowed him to clink his against it. She smiled. He swallowed. Everything was going to be all right.

The crowd that surges back across Park Avenue to Madison between two-thirty and three in the afternoon always looks different from the swarms of the same people going in the other direction at twelve and twelve-thirty. There's a looseness in their walk, especially on a warm spring day when office workers eat their picnics and street-vendor hot dogs lounging around the edges of the splashing fountains in front of the Seagram Building. They hurry out to lunch, remembering errands and making plans, but there isn't such a hurry to get back to work. After three o'clock the change is even more dramatic. The sidewalks are emptier, and a few couples laugh together in their last minutes of stolen time. An occasional lone figure lopes back across the big avenue, tripping on the curb if he was delayed in a bar, or grinning complacently if the delay was a nooner.

"Nooners, nooners," Jack Gilson used to rhapsodize when the subject came up. "Nooners are what make my job worthwhile."

Bristol could never quite believe Gilson's boasting about lunch-hour trysts, but it released balloons of delicious fantasy in his brain. He imagined sidling up to the sexy religion researcher with the big tits and asking her out to lunch, and then he would take her to the Dorset Hotel dining room and over wine he would suggest— Or maybe it wasn't even necessary to ask them out for lunch. Maybe the invitation could be as direct as a hot look over the clipboards in story conference, or a squeeze in a crowded elevator.

He dropped Sherry off at the revolving door into the building and walked down the block to the Montauk Room. Tucked in the corner of a posh midtown hotel, the Montauk was the unofficial meeting place and clubhouse for the magazine's writers and editors. Much of the magazine's real business, and most of its senior employees' complaints, were aired in this dimly lit room of phony fishnets and lobster pots, with big murals of men in Sou'westers around the walls. Franklin Cushing was standing alone, with one of his well-polished English buckle shoes resting on the brass bar rail. His high forehead and beaky nose were silhouetted against a model of a fishing smack.

"Jimmy, get this man a drink," he ordered the bartender as Bristol sat down beside him. Franklin Cushing still got the gentle respect from bartenders and headwaiters that was no longer accorded him by the editors of the magazine. It was odd, Bristol reflected, as Jimmy mixed a perfect martini at the end of the bar: The magazine's founders, the old guard, never would have done a cover story on alcoholism. For them, booze was as much a part of journalism as felt hats and green eyeshades and getting the story and making their deadlines. Franklin Cushing had started in the old days, the days before journalism schools and reporter-celebrities and hundreds of young people babbling about how they wanted to write the truth. Cushing had started on the old *Herald Tribune* in the days when newspaper reporters and editors were people who really did care about the truth, whatever that was—because otherwise there was no reason on earth for them to be there, especially in the case of someone like Cushing, who could easily have starred as a lawyer, or joined his father's brokerage firm.

"How was the Big Fella this morning?" Cushing asked. He had pet names for most members of the editorial staff. Walter was the Big Fella; Barry Rosenberg, a trim suburbanite and Bristol's editor, was the Little Golfer; and another editor, who had a reputation for brutal firings, was dubbed the Axe.

"He killed the paperback story, something happened in Nation," Bristol said. Jimmy's martini wiped out the memory of the rusty-tasting concoction he had drunk at lunch.

"Habib probably has indigestion," Cushing cracked. "Or something of equal magnitude." In leaving Franklin Cushing with almost nothing to do, the editors gave him plenty of time to find ever-wittier ways to make them sound idiotic. He did this very well. Almost as well as he had done his job—when he had one. His jokes amused Bristol, but they also made him uncomfortable.

"It's okay," he said now. "I need all the time I can get for this cover. Bottoms up."

"Have you talked to Sandy Angus over at Roosevelt?" Cushing asked. Dr. Alexander James Angus was a celebrated surgeon and a tremendous power in hospital management—Bristol had already had some trouble reaching him on the telephone.

"I don't think he wants to talk."

Cushing laughed. "A Scot is always a Scot," he said. "Next time you try, tell him I said he'd damn well better cooperate with you. He was in Triangle with me at Princeton.''

''Thanks, Frank, thanks a lot,'' Bristol said. He gave Cushing a brotherly slap on the shoulder and headed out of the bar toward the hot bright sunshine of the waning afternoon.

Back in his office at three, Bristol sank into his desk chair and yawned with satisfaction. In a couple of hours he could start getting ready to go home. The size and furnishings of the room reflected Bristol's status and seniority, just as the size of Walter Sach's office marked his powerful position and the size of Frank Cushing's office indicated his decline. Bristol's door was flanked by two gray metal bookcases end-to-end with two matching file cabinets. A comfortable green vinyl visitor's chair stood in one corner. On the walls were framed tear sheets of each of his cover stories, and the three awards he had won for journalism. Comfortable and private, it was more than a cut above the shared cubicle he had started out in as an apprentice writer. Soon the day would be over. Idly, he flipped through the new pile of messages in his In box. Three of them were ''From the Desk of Barry Rosenberg.'' A small alarm signal started to pulse somewhere in the back of his mind.

''Bill!'' Barry exclaimed into the phone. ''Tried to get you earlier!'' Barry spoke in fragments, as if the extra words that make up a complete sentence were nothing more than a waste of his valuable time.

''I was at lunch,'' Bristol said, to excuse his own elusiveness.

''Extra space in your sections,'' Barry said. ''Need that short on the return of the Hula Hoop before you take off.''

''Sure.'' Bristol groped around the papers on his desk for

the folder containing a few clippings and reports from the bureaus in Chicago and Los Angeles on the new popularity of that demented fad. "I've got the stuff right here."

"About twenty lines." Barry hung up.

Bristol flipped through the pile of files and copy on his desk to find the folder of information on the Hula Hoop story. There were color-coded reports from correspondents in other cities and abroad for stories he was scheduled to write, and copies of his own completed stories in triplicate, waiting to be stored alphabetically in the gray cabinets. The folder was at the bottom. Inside he found a dozen newspaper clippings from all over the country on the fad, and reports from correspondents in Chicago, Los Angeles, and Boston. It wouldn't be a difficult story. He could lead with a joke about the cyclical nature of history, make a few snappy puns, and weave the rest of it around quotes from the correspondents' files; but it would take the rest of the afternoon. Even if he finished the story before five, it would be another hour before Barry edited it. After that, Walter Sachs had to edit Barry's edit. Bristol would be lucky if he made it home for a late dinner.

He rolled a sheet of flimsy copy paper into his big Underwood and looked at his watch. He was certainly going to miss his regular train. He would have to call Julia and explain, and didn't he remember some friction with her earlier in the day, in what now seemed like the distant past? Trouble. There would be trouble about work at home and trouble about home at work. Bristol hated trouble.

Chapter 4

THROUGH THE BEDROOM WINDOW, JULIA COULD see the drooping blooms of the lilac and smell its thick sweet fragrance. It was time to start wearing summer clothes and put away the woolens. In the big oval mirror she admired the way her blue cotton fit over the hips and flared out above the knees. She stepped closer to the glass, buckling a slender leather belt over the inset waist. There were a few new creases on her forehead and around her eyes. She pushed her fingers up against the scalp on either side, drawing her skin taut, and smiled at the younger face smiling back. When she let go, her cheeks seemed to sag off the lines of bone under her eyes and across her jaw—those bones that were supposed to keep her looking sensational in spite of age. Her eyelids looked puffy and she stroked them with the shadow pencil; she used powder to cover a blotch of thread-thin red veins showing above her mouth. Above her lips new wrinkles fanned out like an accordion. In the merciless light from the window, her teeth seemed yellowing and stained. It wasn't fair! Nature had betrayed her, welshing on the promise that she would be forever beautiful, forever young.

Now she stepped back from the mirror and recaptured her old self. From six feet away she still looked trim and elegant. An American Princess, with fine aristocratic features and gleaming golden hair. The buckle of the belt lay flat against her narrow waist, and her slender ankles curved like a dancer's into polished leather pumps. The ankle bone, pressing against her stockings, made a silky crescent above the shoe.

Her high heels clicked on the varnished floorboards. It might rain. She checked the windows in the hallway and Cece's bedroom, and sat down for a moment on the puffy chintz couch in the narrow guest room. The redoubtable Mrs. Griffon had ordered her to get rid of the couch so that they could make the guest room into a dressing room for Cece. Julia didn't see how it could be done, though. The rooms had been redecorated and rearranged ten years ago, and now the door to the guest room was much too small for the big Victorian sofa. Decorators never worried about how. The springs of the couch sang under her weight.

She brought her face close to the fabric to see if it still held traces of her father's smell, bourbon and tweed, or the smoky fragrance of the fireplace in the house on Eighty-first Street. She remembered how she used to love sliding down the smooth rounded back and perching on the wide arms. Sit properly, her mother always said. Billy had proposed to her on that couch, sitting in her parents' living room, and in *their* first house it had held a place of honor under some bookcases, a great old white elephant hand-me-down for a young couple starting out. It looked gigantic and out of scale in the little room, like a silky beast from another age.

She turned the key in the ignition of the station wagon and backed out into the driveway. Pulling the steering wheel to the right, she cut backward to turn around, trying to keep the tires from hitting the edge of the grass. Her father's houses had always had proper places to turn around, even in New Hampshire. Northwood would be strewn with the debris of winter when she got there: maple branches, and coils of birch bark, and the bits of wood thrown down by nesting animals. Next week she would call Darwin Gibbs and ask him to go up and check on the place and turn on the water. She turned left onto Popham Road and slowed down for the Stop sign at the intersection of Elm Avenue. Billy said the Major Deegan was quicker, and Cece favored Route 684, but Julia drove into New York as she always had, down the Bronx River Parkway with its sylvan ponds and rustic bridges, west on the Cross County to Gimbels, and then down the Saw Mill to the West Side Highway.

Popham beyond Elm was still bordered with the broad maple trees and crumbling stone walls of a country lane. Even when Julia and Billy had moved to Ash Hill, there had been a few cows pastured in the fields below the Godwins' big white frame house, and the Sloanes had kept saddle horses. Now the Godwins' barn had been turned into a separate house, and the Godwins had moved away. Cindy

Sloane had gone off to live in Chicago with the children after Jack left her for some girl in his office, and Julia had never met the new family who had moved into their place. The man was a dentist, and she had heard that the Sloanes' wonderful living room and parlor had been remodeled into an office and waiting room with linoleum floors and continuous Muzak.

The road passed the stone steeple of St. Mary's and took a sharp downhill curve at the Henleys' mansard-roofed Victorian. Marge Henley had painted and redone every inch of that beautiful house with her own hands. When Boyd's company transferred him to California, Marge had more regrets about leaving the house than she did about leaving friends and neighbors. At first she and Julia had written each other letters, but now their communication was reduced to scrawled messages on the annual Christmas cards. Beyond the Henleys', the road ran along the tessellated brick walls of the old Bantry estate. It was Charley North's friendship with Julian Bantry that had brought Julia and Billy to Ash Hill to look for a house in the first place. For years the Bantrys' white mansion with its steep roofs and deep porches had been the center of their social world: the yearly Easter-egg hunt for the children, where there was always a prize for Cece, the Christmas Eve party before midnight services, and small, perfectly planned dinners with other favored members of the community. It was ten years since Julian's death; more than five since his widow had moved back to New York City. Now the estate was a New York State center for mentally retarded children. Julia didn't look through the chained gateposts at the house as she drove past.

The end of Popham Road was under construction, and she bumped along on a makeshift surface of concrete, clanging over the slabs of iron that covered the storm drains. At the junction of Popham and Hiller Avenue, she was stopped by a sign telling her to detour to the Hutchinson River Parkway. Julia had no idea how to get to the Hutchinson River Parkway, but she obediently followed the arrows down Hiller and west on Lee Avenue. Turning onto the parkway southbound, she was reassured by the civilized curves of divided asphalt and the big trees on either side. She passed a gas station built to look like a Dutch farmhouse, and slowed down as the parkway curved and doubled back alongside a placid-looking river. In the yards of houses on the opposite side of the water, children were playing and a German shepherd was chained to a clothesline.

But after Pelham the road widened into a confusing mess of exit ramps and extra lanes. As she slowed down to try and pick out the road to New York, a truck behind her honked and rumbled by on the left, barely missing the fender on the driver's side. Without thinking, she swerved to the right and onto a broad cement highway. The pleasant trees and residential streets gave way to a snarl of overheads and bridges as she drove across a bleak industrial wasteland. The road forked again, and when she slowed down, the car behind her honked furiously. Bruckner Expressway. Bruckner Boulevard. Julia's confusion turned to fear as she searched in vain for signs to New York City or the Triborough Bridge. She tried to keep a steady fifty-five miles an hour, but trucks sped by her. An unmarked side road suddenly cut off on the right, and she swung left to avoid it, noticing too late that she had cut in front of another car, a low-slung blue jalopy crowded with men. The brakes screeched as the driver just avoided hitting her. The men were laughing. She veered back over to the right and onto the Bruckner Expressway. At least it sounded fast.

Now the asphalt curved down toward a river, or what was left of one. Dirty water stagnated between crumbling concrete banks. Tenements lined the street on the other side of a rusting Cyclone fence along the edge of the expressway. An abandoned car was upended on the dividing center strip. Every removable piece of metal had been pried off the chassis that sagged on the rims of tireless wheels. Another stripped car had been pushed off to the side; ripped upholstery drooped out of a hole where the door had been, and two wheels were missing. Through the Cyclone fence she saw empty streets and groups of rough-looking men standing on corners. Sullen faces peered down at her from the overpass. The car motor began to make a faint, ominous squeaking sound.

At last a sign pointed right for the Triborough Bridge and New York City. Julia took the turn onto a road that ran along the other side of the fence. Neon signs flashed from a strip of discount-furniture and fast-food places. Plastic banners advertised a carpet-remnant warehouse. She stopped at a red light and noticed two black men standing on the corner. One held a bucket and the other a brush and a rag; a huge transistor radio blaring music was balanced over his free arm.

Julia rolled up her window as the two approached her car. She should have locked all four doors before she left her driveway. One of them slapped the brush full of soapy water against the windshield, obscuring her vision. The other one stared in at her as he rubbed the side window with a dirty rag. As she looked out at him she tried to compose her face in an expression that would be dignified and unprovocative, but her features refused to cooperate. As the first man thumped the back window with his brush, the light changed. She waited until he got around to the other side of the car, and put her foot on the accelerator. There was a curse and a loud thud. In the rearview mirror she could see them gesturing angrily beside the overturned bucket. Now the road curved back down toward the expressway. The squeak in the engine sounded worse.

She was late. Billy would be waiting for her at the top of the steps where they always met. What if he ran into someone he knew? A girl. What if she got there so late that he was gone? She had driven into New York to have dinner with him hundreds of times, but today everything was different. Her old, familiar route was blocked; she had almost had an accident somewhere in the Bronx. Thrown out of her routine, she began to imagine the multiplying possibilities for disaster. When the right lane of the FDR Drive became the exit for Ninety-sixth Street, she had to brake to keep from being shunted off the drive, and the car behind her stopped inches away. Whiplash. A small collision and you had to wear one of those dreadful collars for weeks. Slowing down to fifty, she hugged the side. The road went into the tunnel under Gracie Square and the Brearley School, and leaking water from above splattered on her windshield, obscuring her vision. She imagined the treacherous swirling currents of the East River just to her left. By the time she turned off at Forty-second Street, she was more than fifteen minutes late. Billy would be standing there, handsome and innocent, prey for anyone who happened by. Sherry probably walked with him, just in case. He denied it about Sherry, but that was because he didn't understand women. He didn't know what women were like, and Julia had protected him from that knowledge. She could tell, though, with Sherry and other women he worked with, and even with the wives of his colleagues she had met at parties. He didn't know how attractive he was. Forty-fourth Street was one-way the wrong way; she would have to drive over to Sixth Avenue to get back around to the parking lot. Beads of moisture formed on her forehead, and damp stains spread under the arms of the blue dress. The wetness was unfamiliar, as if she had been changed or wounded somehow.

"You were late, did anything go wrong?" Worry creased the smooth skin over his eyebrows.

"I got detoured onto the Hutchinson, the Bronx River Parkway is closed."

"You should have taken the Deegan," he said. "It's quicker."

"I had to drive through the Bronx. It was pretty terrifying. I don't know why the roads aren't marked better."

"Maybe next time you'll take the Deegan," he said.

"Where are we having dinner?"

"A new French restaurant over on Third Avenue. The great Walter Sachs recommends it highly."

He relaxed and took her arm. Nothing had happened to her. There wasn't going to be any trouble. He looked into her face, and for a moment they gazed blindly at each other, locked away, like two people who have seen in the distance their forgotten dreams, and remembered.

Chapter 5

I F MADISON AVENUE IS AN ARTIFICIAL canyon of glass
and steel with a river of cars running along a narrow rib-
bon of asphalt far below, Bristol's office window was an
eagle's lookout from just above one of the lower preci-
pices—a setback on the tenth floor of the building. From his
vantage point, the traffic and crowds of pedestrians looked
like toys on the floor of some messy and malevolent child's
playroom. The people were always bunched together in
slow-moving mobs, or strung out in a long line at the bus
stop; cars and buses inched along from traffic light to traffic
light on their way uptown.

Across the avenue, on his own level, Bristol could see

into the windows of some offices he had decided belonged to a law firm. It was clearly a prosperous concern, with important-looking ficus plants in the corner office, and framed degrees on the walls of the two next door. Near the middle of the building there was a small room jammed with filing cabinets where a clerk usually sat doing research and where one of the lawyers—men in dark three-piece suits—occasionally appeared for a moment. On the north side, a blonde girl sat in a small reception area decorated to look like a Victorian living room, with flowers in a blue vase on a mahogany butler's table in front of an antique breakfront. She was usually there when Bristol came into his office in the morning, and she never worked late. Sometimes one of the lawyers would still be hunched over his papers at midnight. And when Bristol worked late too, he felt a kind of brotherhood with the man across the street, with their lights blazing while the rest of the lights in the office buildings around them clicked off one by one.

Twice since Bristol had been at the magazine the corner office across from his window had been vacated and redecorated with new shades, new furniture, and even new greenery. The man who worked there now was dark-haired with glasses and wore trim suits on a slight build. Most of the time he sat tilted back in his chair talking on the telephone, or read documents, or dictated to the blonde girl. But some afternoons he would hang his suit jacket over his chair, unbutton his vest, and jump around awkwardly in his business shoes as he shadowboxed with the largest of the plants. Bristol had also seen him take an angry whack at the plant with his umbrella, and throw wadded-up balls of paper at it as he leaned back in his chair during a telephone conversation. Once, on a day that had been particularly boring at the magazine, Bristol saw this lawyer lift his In box high over his head and dump its entire contents on the carpet with gratifying energy. The blonde left the office in tears.

She had her own troubles, as Bristol knew. He had watched her courtship by the law clerk one thrilling autumn. More and more often when Bristol had a minute to spy on them, she would be in the crowded research and filing room, or he would be lounging in the reception area. A few times he saw them leave for lunch at the same time, and he craned his neck to get a glimpse of them leaving the building together from the modern portico ten floors below. The intensity of the flirtation suggested that at least one of them was married; it didn't have that happy air of boy-meets-girl predictability. One evening just before Christmas he saw the consummation of their romance. Under the fluorescent lights, to the sound of recorded Christmas carols from the street, the girl succumbed with her hips up against the low desk in the research cubicle and her legs wrapped around her lover's waist. Unaware of their audience, the couple thrust and pulled back, thrust and pulled back. He imagined their moans, their pleasure, and their final release. Later, when Julia lay underneath him in their bed at Ash Hill, he imagined it again and again.

The fine high bones of Julia's face gazed out at him from a silver frame on top of the office bookshelves. Cece looked blank and pensive in the identical silver frame next to it. They were washed-out studio portraits, and he planned to replace Cece's with a picture that at least looked alive, perhaps even a picture of her as a little girl, instead of this uncomfortable-looking imposter with the carefully page-boyed hair and the mingy smile. There was a third photograph of the three of them together, a happy American family trying to look normal in front of the house at Northwood. But the brooding turrets and the scaly shingle towers dwarfed their figures even in a photograph. Their smiles seemed more nervous than relaxed, as if invisible hands were reaching for them from the dining-room windows.

Charley North had never built that place for ordinary human beings. He had built it for a dynasty, a race of gods. And when Charley and Cecile had been alive, running it like a perfect kingdom with friendly servants and abundant gardens and their beautiful daughter and her beau, they had all felt like gods. Bristol remembered standing on the hill above the pasture late one afternoon and looking down at the house, which was humming with the necessities of human comfort, and the long outbuilding and the lake like a deep-green jewel. Julia had cantered toward him on one of Darwin Gibbs's horses, past the garden and the big balsam in the golden New Hampshire light.

Now juniper bushes blurred the precise edges of the ornamental borders and lily ponds, white pine saplings buckled the clay surface of the tennis court, the slats of the porch were rotting and treacherous; and last summer Bristol had noticed rusting on the iron grille of the cages built for Charley North's private menagerie. There were cages for lions, and pens for wild boars used in hunting parties, and even an elephant habitat—although one of Charley North's few failures was his unsuccessful attempt to acquire an elephant. The old man's obsession with wild animals had begun before Bristol met Julia, on a visit to the Marquess of Bath at Longleat arranged by the ambassador to the Court of St. James's. The great park at Longleat had been turned by its owners into a game preserve, and Charley North was delighted. There were other private menageries in New Hampshire, he soon found out, but he never acknowledged them, insisting on a visit to England whenever he needed advice—or a new lion.

By the time Billy had come to Northwood to court the daughter of the house, Charley had gone on to other projects, and the only inhabitant of the cages was an elderly chimp who later went to the Bronx Zoo. She looked pretty pathetic, peering out from behind the bars and the grillework of the great cages with their special drainage systems and elaborate wood-burning furnaces ordered up from Boston. It was all past history. There had been an intoxicating moment in America when everyone, even middle-class academics like his own parents, had the idea that they could have whatever they wanted, if they worked hard and planned carefully. They were right! It was there for the taking. Both Charley and William Bristol's parents had died before the changes killed their expectations. For Bristol, Northwood was a reminder of what he and Julia *didn't* have, and he sometimes wished she would agree to sell it, or to try a summer on Nantucket or in the Hamptons in an ordinary rental where the present wouldn't be so relentlessly diminished by the past.

Their generation was a generation of lost dreams, he thought. Born after the Depression, they grew up in a time of rebuilding and high hopes, which culminated in the wild optimism of a war that could be won and an economy that provided houses, cars, and free education for all. Although Bristol's parents weren't rich—his father was the head of the English department at a small preparatory school near Boston—it had been taken for granted that they could afford to pay the tuition. They had counted on their ability to support a family on one salary, and on their God-given inalienable right to an architecturally interesting house in a community of like-minded souls. Now that was over. The comfortable margin had been eroded by the sixties, the assassinations, Vietnam, corruption in government, double-digit inflation and soaring interest rates. The men Bristol had grown up with had less money, fewer prospects than their own parents had had. Instead of being hopeful, they were angry.

If it weren't for Julia's inheritance, they would be in the same fix. As it was, Cece, with her average grades, didn't have a chance of getting into Pembroke or Radcliffe, and if it hadn't been for the trust fund they would have had to strain to afford sending her to college at all.

As he walked to the elevator at lunchtime, Bristol's way was blocked by workmen ripping up the old yellow wall-to-wall carpet and putting down a neutral khaki color. Spots made wild expressionist patterns on the rolls of carpeting being pulled off the floor.

There is carpeting in all New York offices. It is always being replaced, but it is still always stained. The carpets are anchored by filing cabinets, and the light is filtered through closed Venetian blinds, or blared from fluorescent tubes. The air is stale but odorless, as if it had already been breathed in and out by hundreds of other people. An imperceptible film of dust, pencil filings and paper molecules settles uniformly over everything, blotting out the individuality that the office workers might once have had.

The back way to the elevators took Bristol past Franklin Cushing's office, and, as he passed, the slim figure in a gray suit joined him in the hallway. Cushing looked oddly lost today, and Bristol guided him forward with a hand on his narrow shoulder. "On your way out to lunch?" he asked.

"One of these days they're going to have to fish me out of the Montauk Room," Cushing said.

"You'll be a record catch."

"They'll probably stuff me and put me under glass, like the trout at Leaders."

Bristol laughed, but he didn't feel like laughing. "William asked for you when I was there last week," he said.

"Good old William. He presided over my father's demise, and now he wants to preside over mine. The club depresses me these days. Too many old men."

The elevator doors opened and they stepped into the carpeted capsule. Bristol was on his way to lunch with Walter Sachs and the chairman of the President's Commission on Alcoholism, a prominent doctor who Sachs thought would be a senator soon. Sachs had insisted that the three of them lunch at Leaders, and ordinarily Bristol would have been happy to laugh with Frank Cushing over their editor-in-chief's eagerness to show off the venerable club. Charley North had sponsored Bristol for Leaders right after Cece was born, and Cushing's grandfather had been one of the club's gentleman founders. Walter Sachs had only been admitted a month ago, and there had been some gossip, deftly passed on by Cushing, about his difficulties in gaining membership.

The Leaders Club was a brick-and-marble building on the west side of Fifth Avenue that Stanford White had designed for its original members, a group of two dozen upper-class trout fisherman. Bristol caught up with Sachs on the broad granite steps, and they entered the polished wooden doors together. A black man in a white coat stood inside in the high-ceilinged marble lobby. "Good morning, Mr. Bristol," he said. "Dr. Rose is on the third floor waiting for you."

"Hello, William!" Sach's loud voice echoed off the inlaid stone floor.

"How do you so, sir," William said.

Bristol walked behind Sachs up the grand staircase to the library. Although Leaders had long ago become a club for aristocrats and their friends—whether or not they could cast a dry fly—the walls were still hung with aging piscine trophies in glass boxes, and cases against the wood paneling displayed the casting equipment and fly-tying genius of departed members. Above them in heavy gold frames hung oil portraits of long-faced men in tackle vests and waders. In the library, a mahogany table was surrounded by deep brass-studded leather chairs where the older members of the club often snoozed away the afternoon. The third floor was the dining room, where tables crowded with silver and napery were attended by silent men in red butler's livery. Bristol savored the otherworldly atmosphere of the club—it was clearly a place where nothing untoward would ever be allowed to happen. But Cushing was right: too many old men.

The President's appointee was seated at a table for three in the corner. Dr. Herbert Rose was a handsome, silver-haired man who had been at Yale Medical School in the great days of Dean Winternitz and Grover Powers. At sixty he had retired from surgery and gone into politics.

"Walter Sachs—Dr. Herbert Rose," Bristol introduced them. "Nice to see you again," he said to Rose. For him the lunch was a formality; Rose had already given him a long interview in his office.

Walter looked reverently around at the dark wooden walls

and fusty oil paintings. "I thought it would be more convenient to lunch at my club," he said. Bristol knew that Herbert Rose had been a member of Leaders for at least a decade. Neither of them mentioned it. Sachs held forth on the changes at the magazine and the improvements in format and content since he had become editor, while Bristol and their guest politely scrutinized the menu. Leaders members considered gourmet cooking to be dangerously effete. Lunch was always chops or steak, spinach and baked potatoes, with fruit or rice pudding offered for dessert. No one in his right mind ever ordered the rice pudding.

"We're delighted in your interest," Rose said, as their lunch was served on plates adorned with the club crest. "It's hard to get serious attention for the problem of alcoholism. Everyone sensationalizes. No one really wants to know about it."

"We're trying to do more in-depth stories, getting further into the infield." Walter carved away at his lambchop as if it were a new problem for the magazine. "You've got a great program at Roosevelt, I hear."

"Well, thank you," Rose said. "We've been very lucky." He turned to Bristol. "Of course your father-in-law gave us immeasurable help. Immeasurable."

"He always wanted his money to make other people as happy as he was," Bristol said.

"A great man. Did you know him?" Rose asked Walter.

"No, I never had the pleasure." Walter sounded cross. Bristol felt he was being held responsible for his boss's failure to have met his father-in-law.

"He would have approved of the changes you've made at the magazine," Bristol lied. Charley would have hated everything about Walter Sachs: his false heartiness, his sports metaphors, his continuous self-congratulation.

Charley had always loved Frank Cushing, and Cushing had repaid him by giving Bristol a job the day he graduated from Brown. "You'll do well," Cushing had ordered as he shook Bristol's hand. And he had been right.

"Charley North was one of those amazing men," Rose went on. Bristol wished he would change the subject. "He knew how to work, and he knew how to enjoy himself. It's hard to tell which is rarer these days."

"I wanted to thank you for giving me so much time last week," Bristol said. Maybe flattery would get Rose onto another topic.

"It was a pleasure, but I'm sure I won't be the most important of your interviews. I understand you even got Alec Angus to talk with you. That's very unsusual. Until now he has refused to talk with the press."

To Bristol's relief, a waiter appeared to clear their plates and take dessert orders, but Walter hardly noticed the interruption. "Bristol's one of the best," he told Rose, talking even more loudly, as if the eminent physician might be too stupid to realize this on his own. "He's the kind of man I'm trying to encourage. That interview with Dr. Angus was typical. I'll take the rice pudding, please."

"I'd still like to know how you got him to talk. Just coffee, please, Arthur," Rose said. Once again the ghost of Frank Cushing hovered over the table. Angus never would have given Bristol an interview without Cushing's intervention. Bristol said nothing.

It was three o'clock by the time he got back to the office. Walter had walked him back down Madison Avenue talking nonstop about how impressed Herb Rose had been with him and his plans for the magazine. Bristol could see that his alcoholism cover was gaining prestige as Walter talked. Now all he had to do was write it. He sank back in his chair and riffled through the first of the stacks of material on his desk. There were piles of clippings, a row of books, and sheaves of reports from other countries. The piece of paper he had rolled into the typewriter before lunch was still there, with his working title printed across it. Alcoholism: Disease or Addiction? Bristol rolled the sheet further down. Someone else had been in his office during his absence. Under his own title they had written another question: "Are alcoholics really sick people, or do they just drink so much because they like to?" Frank Cushing's sense of humor was unmistakable. He was glad the old guy had cheered up.

Bristol twisted in the chair and looked out at the hot afternoon. Across the way in the corner office the little lawyer was bent over his desk in his shirtsleeves. The blonde was at her place in the reception area. The clerk wasn't anywhere to be seen. Bristol thought the blonde looked sad, and he imagined that she might turn around and see him watching her and that he might console her with a smile.

He turned back and rolled a new sheet of paper into the Underwood. Alcoholism: Disease or Addiction? he typed. If he started writing a lead, the story would begin to organize itself. The lead should grab the reader with the importance of the problem; it should make it impossible to stop reading. The classiest lead would be a straight statement of the dimensions of American alcoholism—the numbers, the teenagers and the old people, the fact that it was second only to heart disease and cancer as a cause of death. The other possibility was to lead with a juicy case history from the reports. The decline of an attractive housewife who appeared to have it all. The slide into bankruptcy of a prominent businessman. People loved to read about other people's misfortunes. That was the lead Walter would want. Bristol began to type.

At least today he would be able to leave on time. After Julia went up to New Hampshire at the end of the month the cover deadline would be upon him, and he'd be at the office late night after night. Driving home alone after the last train from Grand Central, to an empty house. He meant it when he said he would miss her.

Chapter 6

JULIA YANKED UP THE COVERS AND pulled the sheet flat, stuffing the ends under a corner of the mattress. There was no point in hospital corners for Billy, he always kicked the sheets off anyway. Writing covers made him nervous. For Julia, Billy's cover stories meant too much toothpaste squeezed out of the tube, and the cap left off, and more clothes dumped on the floor, and even an occasional shattered coffee cup. In another week she would be in New Hampshire, with only herself to pick up after for a while.

Just as she was pulling the bedspread up and tucking it over on itself to make a neat fold for the pillows the telephone rang. Billy was on the train. Cece was still asleep at 5

A.M. in California. She crossed the room and picked up the receiver. Through the wires she heard a faint scratching sound, as if it was a long-distance call. There was a beat of silence, and then a faraway click. It sounded as if someone on the other end had heard Julia's voice and disconnected. Someone who didn't want to talk with her? Someone who wanted to talk to Billy? She put the receiver down and went back to pull the bedspread up over the pillows.

In the bathroom, she re-capped the mangled toothpaste tube and hung Billy's wet towel over the bar along the tub. In the kitchen, she dumped the limp yellow-stained coffee filter out of the Chemex into the garbage pail and rinsed out the hourglass-shaped pot with its worn wooden cinch. It was old, but the new ones had plastic or vinyl waists that looked cheap and cracked easily. There was egg on the plates in the breakfast set, and she rinsed them and stacked them upright in the dishwasher.

As she was sluicing water of the coffee cups, the telephone rang again. She dried her hands quickly on a square of paper towel printed with the powder-blue outlines of vegetables, and reached for the receiver. It could be anyone.

"Hello?" It could be anyone, but it sounded like the same call, menacing her peaceful morning routine. The receiver whistled and scratched as if a great distance was being traveled by sound. A moment passed. Julia was about to hang up when the girl finally spoke.

"Is Bill Bristol there?"

"No, I'm afraid he is not." Julia assumed a cool, authoritative tone.

"Oh." Disappointment vibrated across the great distance. The silence between the two women was as immediate as if they had been in the same room.

"Can I take a message?"

"Well, I'm calling long distance," the voice said, as if that gave it a special power and importance. "I thought he'd be there." Another pause. "Do you think he's at work?"

"Not yet, but I can take a message." Julia held the receiver in both hands, intent on finding out more about the girl and her purpose.

"That's all right. I'll try him at work."

"Can I tell him who called?" The static increased, she had to strain to hear through the layers of noise.

"Well, tell him Terry called, I guess. And if I don't get him at work, tell him I'll see him in New York next week."

"Terry?" Julia asked. Other questions pushed to the front of her mind. But the line was dead.

She went back to stacking the breakfast dishes in the machine. Sometimes the people Billy worked with were bound to call him at home. Occasionally they would probably be calling long distance. These days some of them were bound to be women. She reassured herself, but the burning sensation that had spread across her chest as she spoke to the girl refused to go away. Billy hadn't reached his office yet, but if she called him at work and asked who Terry was, she knew he would have some perfect explanation—whether or not it was true. It was too easy to lie on the telephone. The smart thing to do would be to wait until he got home and she had mixed him a few martinis. Then she could ask him and watch his eyes. And then she would be able to tell.

With this resolve, she headed upstairs to the linen closet at the end of the hallway next to Cece's bedroom. But as she passed the guest room, something drew her toward the soft comfort of the old sofa. It had been so loved, and now it had to go. The idea of losing the sofa seemed unbearable for a moment. Her father's old dog had died at Christmas, there were splits and stains on the furniture her parents had left her, the past was slipping away and the present seemed so difficult. To console herself, she stroked the faded pattern on the big curving arms. Poor old thing. She sat in the corner and stretched her legs out along the cushions. Julia was tall, but her slippered feet didn't even touch the opposite arm. The modern sofas she had looked at in Bloomingdale's were cheaply upholstered, with stingy seats and arms. Everything in the past seemed more generous, easier to understand; and everything from the past was as useless as this old sofa. Lying there, Julia yearned for a time when the virtues of a wife and mother got the respect they deserved, when there were servants instead of supermarkets, when you knew what to expect. She wished for a pleasant daydream, but her anxiety about the girl on the telephone cut into her reverie. She swung her body off the sofa and left the room without looking back.

Downstairs she hitched the carpet attachment to the Electrolux. The sharp whine of the vacuum and the sudden renaissance of color in the old Oriental as the dirt was sucked out of the flat wool should have calmed her. But under the rhythmic roar of the machine the same question formed over and over. Another woman? Another woman? the vacuum asked. In the laundry room next to the kitchen she dumped a pile of his clothes into the washer. Billy's shirts and boxer shorts had a special poignancy now; she examined them for clues. Had he changed somehow, without her noticing it? Another woman? Another woman? asked the swish and grind of the washing cycle.

Upstairs she hung up her nightgown and robe and changed into slacks and a polo shirt. It was warm enough for sandals now. What kind of clothes did Terry wear? she wondered. The name conjured up an image of youth, of liberation, of California girls with the kind of hair-thrown-back laughter that they show in television advertisements.

She imagined a tiny blonde in cheap skin-tight jeans smiling up at Billy. Terry wouldn't complain about Billy's lateness. Terry wouldn't insist on living in the suburbs. Terry didn't smoke, and the skin around her eyes wasn't beginning to crease and puff. It had to be true. In retrospect she recognized the unmistakable signs. A slight preoccupation in Billy's eyes, a waning interest in sex that she had welcomed at the time, the approach of his fiftieth birthday, sorrow over Cece's going away to college. Panic flooded the delicate network of her nerves.

To avoid the telephone, she left the house and sat in the car. There were no errands to run, but if she drove into town something would occur to her. Terry, Terry, Terry, the girl's name seemed to lurk just below the hum of the big station wagon's engine. The little street of shops, with their mock-Tudor façades ending in a neat circle of grass with a perimeter of maple trees, looked oddly artificial and dreamlike. As she pulled into one of the parking places in the lot behind the sporting-goods store, doubt assailed her again. If it was true, and it now seemed inevitably, inexorably true, she had a right to know about it. She crossed the street in front of the Chemical Bank's drive-in window and stepped into the telephone booth on the sidewalk in front of the hardware store.

"I want to make a person-to-person call to William Bristol in New York City, at 212-535-2300."

"Please deposit seventy-five cents."

"Make it a collect call, please." Julia began to perspire.

It was hot in the sealed-off glass booth. Through the panes she saw Ben Lancaster from the desk at the Ash Hill Library coming toward her down Main Street. She turned her face away from him, imagining his glad smile of recognition, his friendly rapping on the outside of the booth, his insistence on buying her a neighborly cup of coffee at the new healthfood restaurant.

"William Bristol's line," a faraway voice said.

"Will you accept a collect person-to-person call for William Bristol?" the operator asked the voice.

Ben Lancaster passed without noticing her, but now she saw Mac the ski salesman's car cruising down the street looking for a place to park. There was a space right in front of the telephone booth.

"Who is calling Mr. Bristol, please?" the snippy voice demanded of the operator. His secretary Sherry, that's whose voice it was. She would probably be listening in when they talked. Julia's heart sank. She couldn't even get Billy's attention to ask if there was another woman without yet *another* woman listening in, monitoring her call, trying to keep her from getting through to her husband.

"His wife," she told the operator firmly.

"Mrs. Bristol," the operator told the voice. The line gave out a series of scratches and clicks. Mac pulled his car into the vacant space and waved to her. She smiled and nodded, breathing a sigh of relief as he walked on past her toward the sporting-goods store.

"Hi, Julie, what's up?" Billy's voice sounded distant and distraced. In the background she heard the rustle of papers being re-sorted and read, and the scratch of his pen as he signed something, or scribbled notes.

"There was a call for you." Her voice sounded shrill and metallic. "I wasn't sure if it was important."

"How come you're calling collect?" At least the idea of an important call had secured his attention.

"I had some errands in town. Does it look like you'll be late tonight?" Maybe she should wait.

"I'm not sure. So what was this important call?" She imagined him picking up the pile of papers again to scan through things while they talked.

"Someone named Terry."

"Terry?"

"She called you this morning."

"I know, I just got off the phone with her. Thanks for taking the message."

"She called you at home."

Billy laughed. "I guess she's a little anxious about filing for the cover. The Hollywood angle of the story is a big job. She's a terrific reporter, but sometimes these girls get a little frantic."

"What was she calling about?" Her voice still sounded high and breathless, as if it were being squeezed out of a box.

"Oh, she was just worried that the second part of her file hadn't come in yet. She wanted to give me some more statistics from a research program they have out there at UCLA."

"You mean she's a correspondent. She works for you?"

"Yeah, Terry Swanson. Are you upset about something? You sound a little strange."

"No." She felt like a diver breaking the surface of the water and taking deep, satisfying breaths of air. Her head seemed light, her body buoyant. "I just wanted to be sure you got the message." She hesitated. "I was a little worried."

"Nothing to worry about," he said. She heard the rustle of papers again. "Did you talk to her at all? She's an interesting girl, her husband's one of the lawyers for the Bank of America out there."

"We didn't talk." There was something else to say, but Julia didn't know what it was. She concentrated on coercing the hazy feeling into words.

"I'll see you later, sweetie," Billy said, and he hung up. Through the glass of the telephone booth she saw Ben Lancaster crossing the street toward her from the newsstand inside Pete's Stationery. She waved and opened the door of the booth, and let the warm spring air slowly fill her lungs. The burning sensation was gone.

"Hi, Ben," she said. "How are things at the library?"

Chapter 7

BECAUSE FRANKLIN CUSHING HAD BEEN AT the magazine for more than thirty years, his farewell party was held in the largest, most opulent office in the building. Walter Sach's office. The editor-in-chief's white sofa and matching armchairs had been pushed against the wall, and his secretary handed a plastic glass of New York State champagne to each member of the staff as they came in. Red and white crepe paper had been looped from the bookcases, over the framed photographs of Sachs with various senators and Vice-Presidents, and down to the drawers of his desk. In one corner, a few desultory white balloons nestled next to the ceiling. A wheel of melting Brie cheese and martial rows of wheat crackers were spread out on a center table near the windows.

At Cushing's insistence the entire staff had been invited, and the room was mobbed with people Bristol had either never seen before or glimpsed only fleetingly in the elevator: glossy young men in three-piece suits from the business side, talking about space rates and ad pages, and the guys from distribution and printing, muscular working-class men in short-sleeved shirts that showed off an occasional tattoo. The room was so crowded that when it came time for the official toasts, Walter Sachs had to stand up on his own desk to say how much the magazine would miss the excellent services of Franklin Cushing, who had done so much in the early days to make it a success. Bristol had the impression that Sachs just barely kept himself from launching into a catalogue of the improvements *he* had made.

When it was his turn, Bristol climbed up on the desk and made a toast about Cushing's humor. And he tried to give the newer people some idea of the scope of stories and ideas Cushing had encouraged when he was in charge. But to Bristol, the party looked like a bad joke. Cushing's popularity, and his sardonic wit about his own predicament, kept it from being the pathetic wake that usually attended "early retirement." Still, there was no question that Bristol's mentor had been eased out. First moved down the hall into smaller and smaller offices, with less and less work to do; and now "invited" to retire at sixty-two and "pursue other interests." Bristol knew perfectly well that Cushing's abiding and passionate interest had always been the magazine. He had no other interests.

Bristol sidled his way through the chattering bodies in the direction of the door, where more champagne was cooling in plastic wastebaskets commandeered for the party. He passed Jack Gilson from business and noticed that he was deep in conversation with Sherry. Maybe she was next on his list. The thought amused Bristol, although it seemed hard to believe that even Gilson found Sherry attractive. Just in case, though, he didn't interrupt them.

Barry Rosenberg was standing at the champagne bucket, and he reached the bottle over to refill Bristol's glass. "How's it going?" he asked.

"I've started the first section," Bristol exaggerated. "It's hard to write about alcoholism without having a drink."

Rosenberg laughed. He had already acquired his summer tan, and he looked as if he was made of something smoother and browner than human flesh. "It's a tough subject for a cover," he said. "The files I've seen look pretty good."

"I see two ways to do it." He might as well find out what Rosenberg thought. That way the editing process would be easier—unless Rosenberg changed his mind. "There's the formal way, leading with statistics and the important stuff—you know, why you should be reading this story. Or there's the human-interest angle. Anna L. was a successful Darien housewife until . . . et cetera."

"I'd go the human-interest route," Rosenberg said. "It's going to be hard enough to get them to read this cover without throwing a lot of information at them right at the beginning."

Bristol considered this advice as he inched through the crowd toward the guest of honor. Rosenberg was right. On the other hand, it was crucial to stress the importance of the problem in the lead. He elbowed through the knot of researchers and computer people surrounding Cushing. Walter Sachs and Rosenberg had already paid their respects, and the party had the feeling of winding down.

"Hey, Frank," he said. "Some party. You're a lucky man to be free." From the look on Cushing's face, he could see that this was the wrong remark. His famous sense of humor was wearing thin. For a moment it looked as if he might tell the truth, but then he recovered himself.

"Leave the place to you young folks," he said. "Martha and I are heading for Nantucket in July. After that I'm thinking about writing a book. A lot of these go-getting book editors have been sniffing around my drawers lately."

"Probably wanted the name of your tailor." Even in this crowd, Cushing was, as usual, the most elegant man in the room, with his high forehead, superbly cut poplin suit, creamy white shirt and blue tie, and polished one-buckle shoes. "What kind of book?"

"Who knows?" Cushing shrugged. "Maybe a memoir, maybe a novel. They don't seem to care, as long as it's a bean spiller." He sounded suddenly weary, but when Angie from the news desk came over to say good-by he squared his shoulders and smiled. Bristol headed through the thinning crowd for the door. It was nice for Cushing to have the opportunity to write a novel, or a memoir, or whatever kind of book he chose to write. Bristol had wanted to write a novel for as long as he could remember. He had begun a few times, but the pressure of his job and paying the bills had made it impossible. Julia didn't like it when he worked at home. At one point he had taken an outline around to a few agents, but they were all discouraging, and the idea that he was only one of hundreds of would-be novelists had depressed him terribly. What was the use, then?

But it would be different for someone like Frank Cushing,

with his connections. And of course, it was no secret that the old man didn't have to worry about money—with or without his magazine job. How would it feel to be slaving away here as a senior editor when Cushing's book came out to general applause and congratulations? Most of Bristol's pieces in the magazine didn't even have his name on them!

The party was ending now, although the room wasn't empty. Sachs and the other senior editors had left, and even Cushing's impressive head had momentarily vanished. Bristol walked down the hall to the men's room, still clutching his plastic glass. Gilson's office was dark, the news desk was being manned by two summer interns, the coils of AP and UPI wire clacking out of the machines lay uncut on the carpet, and it was 5:32 in Bangkok.

In the bathroom, Bristol tossed his empty glass in the bin in the corner and stepped over to the urinals. He was staring at the pale green tiles when he heard the sound above the swishing noise of continually rushing water. It was a low, broken, moaning sound, half animal and half human. Bristol zipped up his pants and whirled around. He had thought he was alone in the bathroom, but now he saw that someone or something locked in one of the two stalls behind him was making this strange, terrible noise. He looked down at the floor below the side of one of the stalls and saw poplin cuffs buckling over two shoes. They were Franklin Cushing's one-buckle English shoes. Bristol left the room quickly and quietly.

Cushing appeared in the door of Bristol's office ten minutes later as he was packing his briefcase. He leaned against the door frame. "I guess that's it," he said.

Bristol was afraid to look at his face. He didn't want to see the red eyes and the quivering chin. But when he did look up, he found that Cushing had composed himself. "It's just the beginning for you," Bristol said. "You're getting out of here." His bitterness surprised him.

"I'll let you know what it's like out there," Cushing said. "Maybe we could have lunch before I go up to Nantucket. I'm a man of leisure now."

"That would be great," Bristol said. "I'll call you." He knew he wouldn't.

Out in the street it was unspeakably hot. The gutters smelled of garbage and the sweet odor of rotting. There was no wind, and although it was after five o'clock, a relentless sun beat down, burning through the shoulders of Bristol's summer suit. He began to sweat. In the street, Mercedes and gleaming station wagons mingled with rattletrap cabs and buses, honking and revving their engines as they stopped and started in the traffic jam going uptown. Clouds of noxious smoke hung over the pavement in the clammy air. The sky was a grayish yellow, and very close. As Bristol walked by Harmon's Coffee Shop, stepping through the blast of intense heat on the other side of its air conditioner, he passed an old man in torn brown clothing shuffling along at the outside of the curb. In one hand the man carried a plastic shopping bag, so old that the original name of the store had been worn off, and with the other hand he waved a half-accusatory, half-accosting gesture.

As he stepped aside to avoid the man, Bristol heard his low, indecipherable mumble. His skin was red and raw, and a torn rag was wrapped around his forehead above watery bloodshot eyes. Naked toes stuck out of his foot coverings of newspaper. As Bristol passed, the man turned his shaggy head to watch him. His skin was dirty and crumpled; his jaws covered with stubble and grit. Rivulets of sweat trickled down the sides of his neck. Bristol kept his eyes on the ground, looking firmly at the concrete in case the man tried to stop him or beg for something. Even in the still, humid air, the bum's septic smell pursued him down the block.

He turned left down Vanderbilt Avenue, past a new bar and a sporting-goods store and the modest entrance to the Yale Club. The blue banner above the doorway hung absolutely straight and limp in the still heat. Bristol's back was wet now; he could feel sweat seeping through his shirt and out to his jacket. His whole body felt swollen. His collar chafed his neck, his waistband cut in, and his loafers rubbed uncomfortably against his feet. As he slowed down for a minute he was passed by another man in a summer suit carrying a briefcase, and then another. They all looked the same, with their Brooks Brothers clothes and their medium-cut hair and their air of hurrying authority. There were thousands of men like him working out their lives in jobs like his. They all wanted to write novels, they all had fantasies about other women, they all hurried back and forth from their office buildings to the station every day. Now the stream of men had become a crowd as he pushed across the avenue toward the Pan Am Building and stopped for a red light. As he crossed, a sudden wind from the rise in the asphalt where Vanderbilt meets Forty-fourth Street hit him with a blast of even more intense heat. Scraps of newspaper flew up and wrapped around his ankles, leaving grimy scars on his trousers. Through his squinted eyes he could see grit blowing toward him in transparent waves over the sidewalk. Below the pavement, the rumble of trains and subways sounded like the groans of men in hell.

Chapter 8

"JULIE DOESN'T HAVE MUCH OF AN EYE," she had heard her mother explain to Mrs. Griffon once in the living room of the house at Palm Beach. Outside the windows there were rows of palm trees, and the garden where cook went for avocados and oranges even though it was winter back in New York. Beyond the garden and across the asphalt road, which was too hot to walk on with bare feet, were the sea wall and the beach where Nanny took her to swim and play on the sand with the shovel and the painted bucket and matching sieve. Her mother was wrong, what she had told Mrs. Griffon was wrong, Julie thought, remembering the flat blue magically flecked with black, of the

66

pupils that stared back at her from the bathroom mirror. She did have an eye, she had two eyes.

But Mrs. Griffon was never wrong. Now she leaned down disapprovingly toward the old Victorian sofa in the upstairs guest room of the house at Ash Hill. Julia had grown up to become the great decorator's client, but time had made no impression on Mrs. Griffon's baby-smooth skin or her domineering disposition. Her immense bosom seemed to be cantilevered off the front of her short body, held on only by the immaculate lace fichu of her blouse. White gloves performed the final gesture of dismissal over the faded blue and red flowers of the old couch.

"You'll have to have it dismantled, then," she responded to Julia's comment that it wouldn't fit out the narrow door. "It has to be out of here before the new furniture comes."

"Isn't there an easier way?"

"I'm afraid not. The easiest way is not usually the best." Years ago it was Mrs. Griffon who had given the orders to put the sofa there. She had even designed the moldings and the new wall separating the guest room from the wide upstairs hallway that now made the sofa impossible to remove. She had chosen every scrap of fabric and furniture in the house, except what Julia had inherited, and she had probably even chosen most of *that* furniture. Nevertheless, she looked around the guest room with a barely concealed disdain, as if some other, far less intelligent person were responsible for all this and as if even she, Mrs. Griffon, would be hard put to set it right.

"All right, I'll get Billy to help with it on Saturday," Julia said as she trailed after Mrs. Griffon out into the hallway and down the curving staircase to the living room. Cece had never liked that big old body catcher anyhow. She had always dreamed of pale pink and creamy satin and goldframed mirrors like in princesses' bedrooms in books of fairy tales. Now she would have them—at least as much as Mrs. Griffon would permit it.

"That will be fine," Mrs. Griffon said, settling in one of the yellow armchairs next to the fireplace and helping herself to her favorite kind of Swiss chocolate, which Julia always bought for her visits. Her tone implied that it wouldn't be a bit fine, but that she, Mrs. Griffon, could see that she had no alternative. "The new couch will be delivered on Monday—it's a satin love seat, *much* more appropriate for a dressing room. Are these Teuscher? I only eat Teuscher."

After Mrs. Griffon had driven away, leaving a trail of instructions behind her, Julia wandered back through the dining room and the living room. It was a bright spring day, and sun pouring through the old-fashioned casement windows made the cherry wood table and side chairs gleam, and blazed away at the lozenges in the blue carpet where it passed the armchairs and the butler's table and the straight brass standing lamp in front of the bookcases. At least the new bedroom would cheer Cece up when she came back for the summer. Lately her voice on the telephone had sounded so sad that Julia desperately wanted to reach through the wires and hug her. She knew that it was trouble with Jerry, although Cece was too proud to say so. Her daughter was from another generation of women, a generation that didn't play the coy games that had characterized her own courting years.

"I have to be honest with Jerry," Cece had said, the one time they had talked about it. "I can't lie and pretend I don't want to see him if I do. What's the point of making him jealous? I love him."

The only trouble was that the coy games worked like a charm, and honesty didn't. Julia was afraid that Cece was too concerned with what was right, and not concerned enough with getting what she wanted. Love was an ephemeral thing, after all, a *frisson* of emotion soon swallowed up in the thousand homely details of two people living together. Why risk losing the man you wanted?

"Come home as soon as the semester is over," she had advised. "leave him flat. He'll start missing you before he knows it." But Cece had already put off her return twice. Sometimes she still sounded like a little girl wanting comforting, sometimes she sounded exhilarated, but when Julia pressed her for dates or suggested making reservations, she sounded as if she would burst into tears. It was clear enough to Julia. The best way Cece could save her relationship with Jerry was to leave him; but she couldn't bear to do it.

Now she was coming next week, she said. If she came, that would be perfect. The rooms would be finished upstairs, and they would be able to go up to New Hampshire together. It would be terrific to have help opening the big house and getting the place in order.

When she told Billy over dinner about the problem of dismantling the old sofa, he seemed unconcerned. Preoccupied.

"Do you think we can do it?" she asked.

"Sure, it's probably just a matter of some cuts in the fabric and loosening a few screws. I'll take care of it Saturday. Could you pass the salt?"

Now he crouched next to the sofa on the floor, which was covered with fragments of wood and scraps of kapok. Drifts of feathers shifted in the breeze from the open window. A crowbar and the big saw were propped against the wall.

Billy raised a sledgehammer over the sofa's back in the attitude of a primitive hunter. The hammer sank ineffectually into the big cushions. The piece looked like an injured beast with one side split open, spilling splinters of bone and viscera into the air.

Julia plunged the carving knife into the fabric on the side of the arm. With the hedge clippers she reached through the hole and tried to pull at an exposed wooden brace. The edge of the big scissors slipped and shrieked as they slid against a metal bolt. Billy levered the crowbar back and the whole frame groaned and sighed. Her father, sitting there in the corner reading the newspaper. She felt queasy as she began a new incision, near where she used to climb up when she wanted to be held in his lap. The blue and red flowers burst open in a final bloom, and a fresh flood of feathers spilled out onto the floor.

"I'll bet a new sofa isn't made like this," Billy said. "Look." The joints had been carefully pegged together without nails, and the stuffing sewn in tiny hand stitches into the fabric in dozens of quilted patches. Billy yanked the patches off, making a long ripping moaning sound, and she could see a cross section of the arm underneath. Fabric and quilting and rubber and wood, all laid down in layers of comfort.

"I adore your mother," her father used to say. There was proof of what he said in the wonderful presents, beautiful things that shimmered on her mother's dressing table or in the square velvet compartments of her jewelry boxes. Rustling silk dresses, flowery perfumes, tiny porcelain lockets, and whole crates of porcelain dinner settings. Later she found out that her father had given presents to other women too. He had managed his affairs as discreetly as he had managed his money. It didn't matter. She would always be his only daughter, his Principessa. And her mother would always be his only wife.

"Why don't you try and loosen the fabric some more with the knife," Billy said. "Then maybe I can knock the back off." Her mother, leaning over her own glittering dressing table in tears. The airy silk of the table's skirts falling around her legs, her twisted face reflected three times by the triptych of mirrors. Julia plunged the knife into the back edge, pushing against the softness with her forearm until the blade clanged against the springs.

Billy braced himself inside the angle of the sofa's ravaged seat, pushing his legs against the back while he supported himself on the bottom. His face was red and he was breathing hard, as if the sofa was a personal adversary wrestling him for a valuable prize. His skin was suffused with blood. What if he pushed too hard? The doctor had warned him against pressure. What if he died, right here in the upstairs guest room? A joint snapped loose with a sharp, explosive sound followed by the scrape and splinter of breaking wood.

"I think it's beginning to give." Billy looped one leg over the back of the seat and raised the hammer again. Suddenly the wood at the sides of the arms began to crack and the back of the seat tilted away at an ungainly angle. It didn't look like a piece of furniture anymore. Billy banged away with renewed force.

"Here we go," he said. "Here we go." Red and intent, his face looked unfamiliar. "Now, that's it, come on," he commanded the dying sofa. He stuck the crowbar between the seat and the back and pushed. The wood cracked with a deeper tearing sound as the two main pieces of the sofa came apart. The fabric ripped open, exposing tiny rows of black springs. Three wooden braces kept the seat and the back from folding together under their pressure. Through the springs, Julia could see the floor of pale-yellow woven webbing that was faintly visible through the muslin on the sofa's underside.

Billy quickly sawed through the wooden structure. When the third brace splintered apart, the whole sofa—feathers, wood, and fabric—seemed to buckle together as if a great hand were squeezing it tight. Billy stood back to admire his work. The wreck of her parents' sofa sat deep in piles of debris, its seat cracked and turned in against itself, jagged wood and strips of the torn webbing hanging from the sides.

"I think we can get it out through the door now," he said. They carried it out the narrow doorway and down the hall to the stairs. It was easy. At the bottom of the staircase Julia stumbled and let go, letting Billy drag it alone to the front door. She watched from a window as he staggered down the driveway pulling it behind him. Tomorrow the Ash Hill garbage truck would come and take it away in the weekly pick-up. Julia walked down the gravel slope with an old sheet from the garage and covered the remains of the sofa where it lay propped up against the mailbox. The wreck was somehow obscene. Under the sheet it suggested a corpse. She hoped no one they knew would be driving by before tomorrow.

Chapter 9

A STAGNANT PAPER CUP OF DELICATESSEN COFFEE balanced on a wad of papers too near the sharp edge of the Formica desk. Behind it a wire basket overflowed with unopened envelopes and press releases, memos, office bulletins, and newspaper clippings. Uneven fans of pink and blue sheets stapled together and datelined Los Angeles, and Dallas, and Rome, were piled on the remaining surface. The window behind the desk was a nighttime mirror image of the chaos, and from the hallway outside the office the high insistent whine of an industrial vacuum cleaner signaled the midnight arrival of the building's professional cleaning service.

Bristol stared at the unresponsive typewriter on the stand at the left side of his desk. His eyes smarted, and all his excess weight seemed to have shifted to his head. He knew that if he kept on instead of quitting, the exhaustion would pass. There was more adrenalin stubbornly hoarding itself in his system; if sufficiently provoked, it would get him through another hour of productive work. The lead, at least, had to be redone before he could leave. With Herbert Rose's caveat against sensationalism in mind, Bristol had originally written a factual lead to introduce his story. The facts were sensational enough. Alcoholism is the first cause of death in the United States after cancer and heart disease. Half of all automobile-accident fatalities and half of all murders are related to alcohol abuse. People with a "drinking problem" are seven times more likely to be separated or divorced than the general population. Ten million Americans are alcoholics.

Barry didn't like it.

So Bristol had written another kind of lead, beginning the story with a series of quick human-interest vignettes. The housewife, nipping away at the sherry bottle all day, asleep when the children got home from school. The businessman, desperately trying to cover up his increasing incompetence, his blackouts, his afternoons at the bar.

The industrial vacuum cleaner reached Bristol's office, and a short man in gray overalls guided the yellow machine through the door, crashing against both sides of the frame. Bristol leaned over his typewriter to avoid conversation, trying to give the impression of being engrossed in his work, although the shrieking noise made concentration impossible. He held himself stiffly upright as the vacuum operator mechanically pushed his machine against the legs of the desk and barely skirted Bristol's loafers with the howling iron mouth. Its tubes rattled and clanked as stray paper clips and staples were drawn into the tank. The man bumped out against the sides of Bristol's office door, and the whine receded down the hallway. The squawk of the intercom shattered the relative silence. Bristol jumped and punched the button that connected him to Walter's office.

"Want to come down?" Walter said.

This meant that Barry had already gone home for the night, and that Walter was planning to leave too. Bristol would be the only worker left in the dark hive of offices, a solitary leftover, typing the night away while the cleaning squad clanked around the building. He pulled out the old lead and made some quick edits, stacking it together with some other material to show what the story would be like.

"Come on in," Walter said. His expensive tie hung loosely in the neck of his expensive shirt. "Toss me what you've got, Billy boy." As Walter read over the pages, Bristol noticed how cheerful he looked, and the pink almost babyish quality of his skin. He imagined his own pallid, deeply lined face; he could feel the crisscross of tiny sore red capillaries in his eyes under the lights. His teeth ached, and an eye muscle beat an involuntary rhythm under his right lid. He hated Walter.

"Good, good job," Walter said. "I think you have it." He flashed his teeth at Bristol and slapped the top of his mahogany desk with his palm. Bristol smiled back. He loved Walter.

"Just a few things . . ." Walter put his head back down to read, and began flapping through the pages. He hated Walter.

"The lead still isn't quite right. It's good, this human-

interest stuff, but we don't want to have it so up front."
Walter was thinking about Herbert Rose. "Try to mix the
facts in sooner," he said, as he drew a red line across the
first page of Bristol's story. "I think the rest will just drop in
the basket for you."

"Okay."

"Let Barry edit it tomorrow. I'll see it again in the final
version."

As Walter tightened the knot of his tie, took his summer-
weight silk blazer from behind the door of his secretary's cubicle, and switched off the lights, Bristol turned and trudged
back down the hall. Walter had passed the story down to
Barry, and this meant that he was basically satisfied and
didn't expect big problems. The end was in sight. Words
and phrases bounced around like manic Ping-Pong balls in
Bristol's head as he eased his soreness back into his office
chair. His heart raced. Too much coffee. He reached out to
move the coffee cup to a safer place on the windowsill, and
took a swallow. It was brackish and cold. Under the fluorescent light, the crescent shape of a stain on his carpet was like
a new summer moon.

He typed the first line of the new lead on the blank piece
of paper. Barry wouldn't like it. He had to find some way to
start with the human-interest stories without giving them too
much importance. In an hour he'd be going home anyway,
driving up the expressway through the night air. The last
train to Ash Hill left Grand Central at midnight, so when he
was going to be late he drove the little car into the city and
drove home after work—once even right into the dawn leaking up out of Long Island Sound as if a huge balloon filled
with paint had exploded just below the horizon.

He was afraid of falling asleep at the wheel. Some nights

it was a struggle all the way to keep control. First he would turn the car radio up so loud that his ears ached; and when they began to go numb he would turn the radio off and try to sing, breathing as deeply as he could. Songs from his childhood, and Christmas carols, and hymns, and old college songs.

"We are always true to Brown, and we love our college dear," he bellowed as he guided the car under the bridges of the Deegan and onto Route 287 in the seductive air of the summer night.

"And wherever we may go (we may go)" he growled out the syncopation, "we are ready with our (ready with our) cheer.

"For the people always say (What do they say?)

"That you can't outshout Brown men (not Brown men)

"With their rah, rah, rah, and their whiskey clear

"And their bee are o double-you ennn. (Rah, rah, rah.)"

By the time he got off the parkway and onto the local roads, the struggle had intensified. He stopped on the ramp to Popham and slapped his cheeks, shaking his head to dislodge the delicious fuzzy caul of sleep. His eyelids seemed to have an independent life, beyond his control.

One dawn he had awaked with a frightened start to find that he had driven off the road, the car tilted half into the storm gutter with the front end pointing into the creek that ran along the edge of Lake Avenue. He couldn't remember dozing off, but suddenly he was wide awake and terrified. He might have driven right off the bridge; he might have driven right into one of the concrete stanchions.

The next morning was overcast and hot. Bristol slowly turned the faucet until the water was almost scalding him.

His skin turned red where the drops beat against it, and waves of steam billowed off the hard stream from the shower head. Then he twisted his wrist back, yelling with a shock that he was never quite prepared for as the water changed to an icy sluice that ran through his hair and down his spine. In the kitchen he filled the Chemex filter to the brim to make opaque brown coffee gritty with grounds. While the water boiled, he took three of Julia's vitamin tablets and three aspirin from their containers on the shelf. Back in the bathroom he shaved, cutting himself twice and stanching the blood with bits of Kleenex—they'd be off before he got to the city. Flat gray light came through the bedroom curtains as he dressed. Clean this, clean that, and the comfortable chinos and polo shirt that writers were traditionally permitted in the final days of a cover story—although they had better look as trim and neat as a suit.

At the office he got the special treatment that writing covers is the price for. They were either tearing you apart or treating you like some kind of pompous Pooh-Bah, Bristol thought. He missed Frank Cushing. A card from Nantucket was tacked above his desk. "Wish I was here," Cushing had written.

The day was filled with the sound of his own typing. As he worked, the solution to the problem of facts versus human anecdotes came to him. He would italicize the anecdotes, beginning with the strongest one and sprinkling the rest of them through the story. He ticked off the information blocks in his outline, and piled statistics and facts into each paragraph. History. Definition. Damage to the individual. Damage to corporations and the economy. Symptoms. Women (this was a special section). Treatments available. A sidebar quiz: Are you an alcoholic?

At five o'clock, he slid the pile of pages off his desk and straightened the edges by knocking the side of the pile against the Formica. After printing his last name and the cover-story code number on the top, he carried it down the hall to the copy desk. In an hour, the computers would print and distribute a dozen copies to each of the senior editors at the magazine. No matter what Barry did to it later, his original version would be read by everyone before it was edited. Bristol often imagined that his original story would be so clear, so stunning in its rightness, that Walter would decide that it didn't need any editing at all. In this daydream, Walter came into Bristol's office waving the story in his hand and raving about its perfection. Then Walter would tell Barry not to edit it, but to let it run the way Bristol had written it.

He ordered a roast-beef sandwich from the stained takeout menu of the Madison Avenue Delicatessen, and when the voice taking his order paused, Bristol added two beers, a side of French fries, and a piece of cheesecake. He deserved it. He knew that down the hall Barry was reading the story, deadly red pencil poised and ready. He imagined Barry smiling with pleasure and approval, chuckling to himself and letting the pencil drop as he read. He imagined Barry's face crunched into a frown as he cut and slashed with the pencil, and finally just put it down because the whole story would have to be redone and there was no point in editing it.

It would be over tomorrow, whatever happened. He would get some sleep, and pack, and then drive north out of the heat and away from the noise of jackhammers and traffic and the smell of gutter rot. He would lie on the grass under the maple trees near the cage building and listen to the peaceful *whirra whirra* of the summer morning. He would help Julia with the lawns and the repairs, and swim in the lake with Cece. He saw the eerie white flash of her legs underwater as he dove from the dock, and felt the cool springs from the fine sandy bottom that surprised him as he swam ashore.

The intercom buzzer summoned him to Barry's office. As he walked in, Bristol could see the printed pages of his cover spread out on Barry's desk and scrawled with cryptic notations. He caught a glimpse of one page with a big red question mark next to one of the italicized anecdotes.

"I think the lead is just fine," Barry said. He didn't look up. "It needs a little recasting later on, though." (This was an editor's euphemism for a total reorganization.) "I'm not sure that you don't get to the point too fast. (That was a polite way of saying that Barry didn't agree with Bristol's conclusions.) "I think you need to flick in more stuff from the files here and there." (This was an editor's way of demanding at least a dozen new quotes and facts knitted into the story from the out-of-town reports.) "And the writing is a bit dry in places." (Furthermore, he didn't like Bristol's prose style.) "Otherwise, it's a good job," Barry said.

"I thought italicizing those anecdotes was a good way of getting the human story in without sensationalizing it," Bristol said. "That's why I organized it that way."

Barry hummed a low, negative note. Bristol could see him weighing the truth—the story had to be rewritten—against the value of keeping Bristol happy so that he would do it without a fight. "I'm not sure that italicizing really works," he said. "It's a little distracting. The anecdotes are too personal and the other stuff is too factual. I think when you've shifted the organization a bit you'll find you don't need to do that." It was going to be a long night.

Bristol leaned over the Underwood, the roast-beef sandwich uneaten at his side, his desk covered with the salvageable pieces of the cover. His back hurt. Scissors, Scotch tape. His eyes red, his clothes rumpled, and his cowlick upended, Bristol consulted twice more with Barry before Barry left for the night. The whine of the industrial vacuum cleaner filled his office as he wrote, and the machine's operator bumped it against his bookshelves and the door frame. For a long time he worked alone in the building, catnapping on Barry's couch when he got too tired to type. As the night outside turned to gray and then yellow he finished. It was about nine in the morning, and other people, people who had gone home for the night, were beginning to come into the office when Bristol dropped the rewritten cover onto the copy desk.

It was done now, anyway. Written, edited, and rewritten ready to be sent on its way to the copy department and on to the printing plant where the great presses clanked and rolled miles of paper off their webs, to the distribution warehouse piled with twine-bound stacks of magazines, to the city newsstand on Eighty-sixth Street where an old blind man would clip it to the front of his display case, to the swanky magazine racks in the stores on Rodeo Drive in Beverly Hills and North Michigan Avenue in Chicago, to the doorsteps in the suburbs of San Antonio and Memphis, and to rural mail tubes, lonesome stalks of communication stuck in the flatness of the midwestern prairies, where farmers would drive up in pickups and pull it out late in the afternoon after the cows were in.

Exhaustion blurred Bristol's movements as he cleared off

the pyramids of paper accumulated on his desk. In an hour the new cover would be printed, and then Walter could okay it and Bristol could go home. He would lie on the soft grass in front of Northwood and look down at the lake and over through the woods toward the garden. The air would be clear and sweet. In the distance he would hear the peaceful clinks and scrapes of Julia fixing his lunch in the kitchen.

A slight sound pulled Bristol out of his dream. Walter was standing just inside the door of his office, his briefcase in one hand and his copy of Bristol's original story in the other. Bristol remembered to smile.

"I'm just on my way in," Walter said. "I wanted to stop by and tell you. It's a terrific cover. Good job." He waved the printed pages for emphasis. The rejected sections of italics winked out at Bristol. "Good job," Walter said, again.

"Oh, thanks. Barry suggested some changes."

"Minor, minor, you did a great job."

"Well, that device of italicizing didn't seem to work."

"I thought it was perfect. Got the ball right onto the fairway. See you later." Walter executed a splayed-finger semisalute indicating his own intense busyness, and vanished down the hall.

Bristol swiveled in his chair and stared out the window. Across the way, the workers in the law firm were just coming in for the day. The man in the corner office rushed into his room carrying a steaming mug of coffee. The blonde secretary followed, holding a stack of pink telephone-message slips. The man hung his blazer on the hanger behind the door and picked up the receiver of his telephone as he sat down. The secretary put the pink slips in his wooden In box and then stood waiting for further orders. She stared at the ficus tree in the corner, but her eyes never moved the millimeter to the right that would have brought Bristol into her line of vision. He turned back to his own dilemma.

That was the highest, most effusive praise Walter had given anything he had written in four years, and it was praise for his original cover story! Bristol let the numb weight of his shoulders sag toward his hips. In spite of the men's-room sponge bath he had taken at dawn, he could smell his own sweat. But Walter had been talking about the *original* cover that he had taken home with him last night—not the rewritten cover that was even now being prepared for his final okay.

As the morning went by, Bristol's satisfaction (he was right, it was a good cover, Walter said so) engaged his increasing nervousness (Barry would be furious, the whole thing would have to be redone again to incorporate the new cover and the old cover, another day, another night) on a broad inner battlefield. He heard the screech and grind of hopes meeting opposite hopes, the terrible clash of ideals and practical details. It would be wonderful to have a cover that he was proud of in the magazine. It would be horrible to have to work another night.

The wet patches on the back of his stale polo shirt began to turn icy in the morning blast of air conditioning. Across the way, the corner-office lawyer was leaning back in his chair, limning relaxation as he talked to another man who sat upright in the visitor's chair. At lunchtime the secretary opened the white wrappings of a sandwich at her desk, and pulled the tear-shaped metal tab off a can of soda. Wouldn't it be nice to be a law clerk or a secretary? You did your work. You collected your paycheck. That was it.

After the corner-office man left for lunch, Bristol passed the minutes by reading the *New York Times*. Halfway through he realized that he couldn't remember anything he had read. He started again, forcing his eye down each column, ticking off the facts. The President's foreign policy. The unseasonable heat. The increase in the New York City unemployment rate. The inexplicable boom in book buying. Keeping his eye off the door and his thoughts off the telephone, he bent his attention to each page. Sherry brought him some more coffee and a turkey-salad sandwich from the lunch wagon. Men's fall fashions showed less construction in the jackets, longer trousers, narrower ties. In ninety percent of cases diagnosed as senility, the problem turned out to be something else; an allergic reaction, or depression, or an overwhelming sadness. Bristol felt an overwhelming sadness. He wanted to cry. In sports, the baseball season was underway; and he tried to concentrate on a long piece on home repairs. What is the best way to reglue broken antiques? The use of a vise. Bristol felt as if he were caught in a vise. It was two o'clock by the time Sherry brought him the final copy of the cover, with a message from Walter.

"He says you should just read this over and then you can go," she said. A note was pinned to the top of the pages. "Nice job. See you in September. Barry." It was the edited rewritten version, complete with the long inserts from the files and the clumsy weaving together of personal and factual. No classy italicized anecdotes. No reasonable factual presentation of the problem. Herbert Rose would think it was sensationalism. Most people would be a little bored. Bristol turned to the top of the page. There were Walter's initials and his scrawled OK. That was it then. He could go. With a jolt of disappointment, he realized how much he had wanted them to tear the day apart and insist on printing his original cover. Once more he imagined readers picking the magazine up at the Eighty-sixth Street newsstand and on Rodeo Drive, and pulling it from the mail tubes of the midwestern wheat country, enjoying the cover he had been so proud of. The anecdotes would have drawn them in, the facts and figures would have opened their eyes.

Walter's big head appeared disembodied around the doorjamb. "Just give that a read and have a good vacation," he said. His ruddy outsize features were blank; no acknowledgment, no confusion.

"Thanks," Bristol said. Maybe he was mistaken. Maybe the covers were about the same. Had the first one really been so much better? So much different? "Thanks," he said again. And with an inner release that felt like a stretched-out band of thick rubber easing and snapping open, he pushed his tired cheeks upward in a smile.

Chapter 10

THE WHEELS OF THE STATION WAGON spun in the dirt and gravel at the edge of the road, deepening the ruts and sending plumes of earth flying in both directions. She had overloaded the back. Each turn of the steering wheel brought a fresh crunch and then the familiar whine as the spinning tires settled in. Over the pine trees on the right she could see the roof of the house, but it was still half a mile away. She was stranded with nobody to help her, sinking in the shoulder of this remote back road with no one for miles around.

Through the windshield, Julia could see the stand of birches ahead where the driveway to Northwood began; in

the rearview mirror, a solid mass of pine trees. If she tried
going into reverse to get out of the ruts on this grade the car
might slide over the road's edge and down into Hemlock
Brook. They might not find her for days. Panicked, she
jammed her foot down on the accelerator, and the car leapt
forward out of the ruts and across the road toward a big maple tree on the other side. Its arms reached out to welcome
the car, to crush its metal body against the scaly trunk. Julia
veered away from it up the hill, and brought the car back to
the center of the road. If anything happened up here she was
completely isolated. They might not find her for days. She
eased the car up the rest of the road in first, and turned into
the driveway. Anything might have gone wrong with the
house during the long New Hampshire winter. An electrical
short could have started a fire, and she would find the south
wing a charred skeleton, with black bones propping up the
rotting walls and sheets of mildew hanging from the beams.
One of the big maples might have come down in a storm,
leaving a line of crumpled wood and glass through the middle of the living room. The weight of the January snows
might have collapsed the old roof. Pipes frozen, wires
snapped in the freezing nights. Darwin Gibbs from the village had already been up to turn on the water, as he did
every June 15, and Julia tried to reassure herself with the
thought that he would have called if anything was wrong. It
didn't work.

As she'd driven over the rolling hills south of Danbury,
Connecticut, she had imagined the rooms stripped by
thieves, drawers hanging open and empty frames askew on
the walls. A vivid flash of a grisly corpse left to rot in the
potato bins assailed her as she turned off Route 86 and onto
the Massachusetts Turnpike after Sturbridge. Later the steep

banks where Route 93 had been blasted through the piny New Hampshire midlands suggested that the hills around Northwood might have eroded, cracking the fieldstone foundation, knocking through the septic tank, or sending boulders from the top of the hill down through the vulnerable white wooden skin of the house.

But there was no evidence of major destruction as she pulled the car into the circle of drive at the end of the road. Branches and brush blocked the way, and she had to get out and drag a peeling dead birch limb off to the side to get into her habitual parking place opposite the front door. Darwin Gibbs' recent footprints marked the nine-months' accumulation of debris and dust on the front steps. The lock thumped as she turned her key and the door slowly opened under the weight of her right shoulder. Light filtered into the downstairs living room through the closed shutters, giving the place the eerie quality of somewhere underwater. The furniture under white winter drop cloths loomed up in the dusk like strange rocks and corals.

The room seemed oppressive and airless, a stagnant atmosphere laced with the must and cobwebs of empty days and empty nights. Julia's footsteps creaked on the floorboards as she crossed to draw back the curtains, open the windows, and push the shutters back against the house, where they hooked to anchored metal S curves. Their hinges shrieked in reproach at the hours she had left them untended, the seasons that had come and gone unnoticed, the nine months of neglect.

Through the door of the downstairs study, the light fell on the broad mahogany desk where her father had once held court. Someone seemed to have been there a moment ago. Now the room was empty. She could see that the sheaves of paper she had forgotten to clear off after Billy's attempt to write a short story last summer had already been made into nests and tunnels by the field mice, who came inside through uncaulked gaps in the foundation when the temperature dropped in the fall. An imperceptible sound drew her eyes to the small window at the landing of the staircase up to the second floor. A face had been looking through the glass, but it vanished when she turned toward it. In the downstairs bathroom a dead mouse and the six tiny skeletons of the litter she had delivered there huddled trapped in the bathtub just above the drain.

In the corner of the living room, an old mahogany plant stand of her mother's leaned at an odd angle against the sofa. Julia reached out to right it, and the wood split apart into three pieces. The cold had finally warped it past endurance. She cradled the splintered pieces in her arms and took them out to the kitchen. Every summer morning her mother had gone out to the cutting garden, an old-fashioned woman in a broad sun hat carrying a flower basket and shears, to get the gladioli and zinnias and roses for the arrangement that always sat on the mirror finish of the stand's top. Now pieces of broken wood. She wouldn't throw it out right away. It could go in the tool shed; maybe someone could fix it.

Leaning down to grab the edges, she pulled the white drop cloths off sofas and chairs, folding them into neat rectangles for the bottom of the linen closet. The fabric seemed to cling to the furniture, and her lungs filled with the minute particles that settled through the long shafts of light onto the carpet and her clothes and hair. She kept a watch on the curve of the staircase as she uncovered the last of the set of Queen Anne side chairs, and when she carried the bags of groceries and household necessities in from the car to the kitchen, she looked up at the landing after each trip. It was ridiculous to think that anyone was up there. A chip of wood, jarred by her footsteps, fell off the dining-room table's protective cloth and chattered across the surface of the floor.

At the front door she gulped in sweet air from outside the thick chill of the house, as if the rooms really were underwater and she had been drowning. Malevolent nature was trying to undo all her work, sending the elements to disintegrate the noble ruins of what her father had built. Some powerful, unspeakable force was working against her to reclaim it. She was fighting the numberless animals, the thousands of tons of weight of the winter snows, and the freak violence of the mountain storms when jagged lightning zigzagged back and forth across the valley, igniting roofs like tinder, sending wild fireballs through open windows, and striking sparks off the lightning rods strung along the roof ridge.

After one winter there was dust everywhere. The beds and floors were covered with debris and the messes left by dead mice and bats; porcupines had eaten holes in the wooden part of the foundations, and birds and raccoons had strewn enough bark and branches to kill the lawns around the big trees, if they weren't raked. The few remaining garden borders were matted with weeds, the grass near the house was high and going to seed, and in the meadow dozens of maple and oak saplings had taken root—ready to grow up into scraggly second timber.

After two winters, if she didn't come, there would be a more dangerous mess. A broken window where the snow had come in and melted into puddles, staining the furniture and rotting the floor. After three winters, the roofs would begin to leak. In the spring, the water from the melting snow and icicles would drip inside, dampening the insulation and invading the inner walls. The saplings in the meadow would be as high as a man by then. After that, there would be more broken windows, holes in the shingles and the floorboards of the porch, little gashes in the interior walls where the wasps would nest and the animals come indoors. Soon the roof would begin to cave in and the weeds and brambles would have their way with the lawn, and the walls would begin to crumble toward the meadow. All that would be left would be the stone foundation, a few rusted pieces of equipment, a few old boards, standing in a part of the forest that seemed a little less dense.

Maybe there had been a pasture there once, people might think if they came on it during a summertime walk through the north woods. There were lots of foundations like that in New Hampshire. Old cellar holes with walls still sagging above them, or stones covered with ivy and honeysuckle, abandoned places where families had eked some kind of living out of the stony soil, scraping at the granite and building stone walls as boundaries and fences for the stock. There were stone walls all through the New Hampshire woods, even up near the tops of the hills, miles away from any surviving farmhouse.

Chipmunks and hedgehogs nested in those walls, and her father's old Labrador used to race after them with his fat black tail upright in excitement. He would trot along nose to the ground, or carefully stalk a chipmunk as it sat under a tree. With a whine he would break and chase after it, sometimes coming to a sliding halt just in time to keep from knocking himself out on a stone wall as the rodent disappeared between two rocks. Even last year he had been there.

Limping with arthritis and drooping with age, he still remembered everything, and roared into the house with his grizzled head high, as if he expected to see his master any minute. He pranced through the living room and up the stairs, checking each room and hallway with his nose to make sure his doggy kingdom was in order. When the vet had told Julia that Sandy was too old to keep alive, that last time, and the dog had obediently shuffled out of the linoleum waiting room, led by a leash to his death, she had thought they would buy a new dog. But a dog was such a lot of trouble. Dog hair on the rugs and dog doo on the lawns and inexplicable holes in the flower garden. Now she wished they had bought a new one anyway. The empty house trembled with chilling possibilities.

The door to the pantry was ajar. Julia pushed it open and stood back, but there was nothing unusual inside. Shelves of canned goods and a few bottles of liquor flanked piles of dinner plates, salad plates, soup plates, and cups and saucers, all in her mother's blue and gold Wedgwood with the tiny raised crowns along the edge. She blew the dust out of a highball glass from the shelves of crystal that formed a right angle along the other wall, and poured in four fingers of Scotch from a half-empty Dewar's bottle. Six hours was a long drive. There was still a lot of work to be done. She splashed an extra measure of Scotch into the glass and walked outside.

The evening's colors as the sun cascaded its last beams across the lake spread out like a rainbow. Light prismed through the gold in her glass, and she leaned against the wooden balustrade surrounding the big porch. The pasture needed mowing. The trees on the other side of the stables should be topped. Even from here she could see that the winter storms had displaced some of the boards in the dock that jutted out into the glassy water of the lake from beyond the green roof of the boathouse. Mountains rose steeply on the other side, eclipsing the sun as it set and giving the air a steely northern edge.

Below her on the south side of the pasture, the stables and the menagerie looked as if they had survived the winter intact. Soon they would need paint. Last year, after he had spent a week fixing the leaks in the wall of the elephant cage, Darwin Gibbs had come to her with his soiled, dark-green farmer's cap bunched up in his hands, and suggested that it was time to tear them down. They didn't keep horses anymore, and there was certainly no need for those cages for wild animals, "if you know what I mean, Ma'am." It wasn't really worth keeping them up; they could be dismantled, and the fancy iron grillework around the cages was probably worth a bit, if they cared to sell it. She told him no, she didn't want the buildings to come down yet; and she wondered if he had cooked up a deal to sell the grille in the village or down in Concord. If there were more repairs to be made this year, she would get Billy to do them.

Indoors she wiped the winter's accumulations out of the cast-iron frying pan and dumped last-summer's crumbs out of the toaster oven. She took bread and eggs out of the refrigerator. It was plugged in again and humming along fine, but it would have to be thoroughly cleaned. And she had another whiskey. It was dark. When she pulled the chain on the standing lamp next to the couch in the living room, the bulb flashed out with an explosive pop. Tomorrow she would have to check all the bulbs.

The dining-room table was still covered with a fitted cloth—protection for the shiny finish that had often showed her back a little-girl's grin and an instant double chin because she was looking down at it. She set a place for herself at the flecked Formica table near the stove, with a stainless-steel fork and a limp paper napkin. The two eggs slid neatly out of their shells and onto the shiny black surface of the pan, and when their white edges started to flap and bubble in the butter, she pushed down the two slices of wheat-germ bread in the toaster. When the toast was up and the pieces lay side by side on one of the white kitchen plates, she slipped a spatula under the eggs and with perfect precision deposited an egg on each slice. Her parents had probably never eaten eggs and toast after noon in their lives, any more than her father would have worn a tuxedo before six in the evening. As a girl in this house, she hadn't even been allowed in the kitchen. "Hi, Princess," Leona the cook would say when she craned curiously around the edge of the doorway before lunch.

Her fork punctured the egg yolks, and the yellow liquid oozed across the neat symmetry of her dinner. Once Julia had been the little Princess in this palace of a summer house, now she sat alone over a slapped-together dinnertime breakfast, under the hostile glare of the fluorescent lights, a Princess unattended, eating a cheap meal off a tinny fork. She began to cry.

Chapter 11

I T WAS ALREADY ELEVEN O'CLOCK IN the morning by the
time Billy turned down the curving exit ramp off Route
684 and got onto 84 going through Danbury toward Hartford. The tires bumped along the skid-prevention ruts in the
asphalt. He was late. If Julia had made lunch for him her
feelings would be hurt. By watching the speedometer and
stopping just once he could probably get there in time for an
afternoon swim, though. The transparent green water would
fold around his sweaty skin, feeling icy for a moment because it came into the lake from the mountain snow and the
streams that ran down to it through granite and moss. He
would take a last gulp of air and then plunge underwater,

letting the distilled cold caress his scalp and inside his ears and between his toes, and wash away the grit and trouble of the city.

There was highway construction near Waterbury, where the road curved around a knob of rock that was a tourist attraction called Holy Land and a cross stood out against the sky. He idled in the traffic, inching toward the point where three lanes of cars merged into one, and looked out over the brick towers and warehouses of the town. Noon heat assaulted the top of the car and radiated down toward him. His shirt was wet against the vinyl of the driver's seat. He was late.

Beyond Hartford the road narrowed and became a crowded four-lane strip divided by a dented guardrail. Trucks rumbled by him, the huge undersides and axles passing almost at eye level, their backdrafts pushing his little car toward the shoulder. The air smelled of scorching asphalt and diesel fumes. At Northwood he would mow the lawns and breathe in the fragrance of the cut grass where it fell in downy rows to either side of the whirling blades as he was pulled along behind the Fruehauf. He would sharpen the scythe on the whetstone in the tool shed and do the pasture, throwing himself forward into the rhythmic ancient motion of the curved blade as the long grass fell in sweet-smelling rows. Last year he had noticed that the wood at the back of the interior walls in Charley's menagerie building was buckling and splintering; he would buy new wood at the lumberyard in Granville Center and replace the boards. He heard the regular, calming sound of his own hammer, and felt the neat satisfaction of reaching into a number-nine nail keg and finding a number-nine nail. The acrid paint smell would invade his sinuses, and sawdust would pile up around his workboots.

The practical answer for that menagerie building was to tear it down. The wrought-iron grilles could go to a museum or be auctioned at Sotheby's. Charley had brought a man over from Italy to create them as a decorative scrim for the bars of the cages. Giuseppe from San Gimignano, a little leathery old man who always wore a blue worker's smock, had set up an anvil and a smithy in the old woodshed, and magically twirled a pile of straight iron girders into the graceful minuets of laurel and ivy, twined around fanciful animal figures, that stood in the building's dim light. It had taken him two summers, and the entire household had picked up a smattering of Italian phrases that Charley insisted on using in Italian restaurants, to everyone else's embarrassment, until the end of his life.

"Che cosa de speciale, oggi?" he would say, in a flat upperclass accent that was right out of Princeton in the twenties; or "Il conto, per favore." The waiters would roll their eyes while Cecile pretended not to notice, and try to answer politely without smiling, because Charley North was always a very important customer.

That iron grillework, those cages, were the irreducible remnants of a time before taxes and inflation had finally eroded what used to be the privileges of the rich—or the rich who had any style. They could have anything. When Charley had visited Longleat, there had been no question about his ability to create his own menagerie. But it wasn't just money. Those were the days when good manners and a gentleman's word and an Ivy League education really stood for something. The days when a man like Frank Cushing was appreciated by everyone, not by just a few holdouts. Billy slowed the car as he approached the toll booth at the entrance to the Massachusetts Turnpike. A sour-faced man in a rumpled green uniform handed him a computerized ticket.

Nostalgia stayed with him as he accelerated onto the wide concrete strips of the pike. What a life Charley and men like Charley had had in those days! There were gala sailings on the *Mauretania,* and trips to Europe that looped from castle to schloss to chateau and back again, with stops for important shopping in Rome and Paris. Charley had been so fascinated by cars that he bought almost every model and make the moment it came on the market. By the time he settled on the Buick, he had bought and sold twenty-five automobiles. Charley's rich friends had yachts and houses with sweeping lawns and dozens of servants: shy lasses from Donegal, and crisp tyrannical nannies from England, and Italian gardeners in berets, and black men with soft southern accents who dressed in uniforms and spent hours polishing cars with creamy chamois cloths. Charley's poor friends had to go and live in the south of France.

He stopped for coffee at the first Howard Johnson's on the turnpike. Steering the car around the gabled reconstruction of the Massachusetts Bay Colony cape house that housed the Tourist Information Center, Billy parked at the end of the curb behind the building. Through the glass he could see the burly forms of two truckers as they slurped at pink and white ice-cream sodas in tulip-shaped glasses. A woman in a purple blouse with her hair set in exact, symmetrical rows of curlers was waiting in the takeout line at the counter. Behind her another woman, her curlers outlined under a patterned head scarf, licked at a bright-green cone. A little girl in a Boston Red Sox T-shirt pulled at her free hand, straining toward the cases of silver-wrapped candies and

Howard Johnson frozen dinners. Outside the doors to the restaurant, Billy passed a young boy in tears. He was pulling his white T-shirt away from his small chest as he wept, gazing through the glass as if in exile from a world of treasures.

"You can go in," Billy told him, stooping down to the boy's level as he opened the door. "Come on."

"Get in here, Eddie!" The voice of the woman in the scarf pierced through the background noises of cars and trucks and people talking and transistor radios blaring the deep bass beat of rock. She reached out and yanked the little boy into the restaurant, bumping his body against Billy's in the process. The door that Billy had been holding open slammed behind her in his face.

Inside, he turned left down the long corridor to the men's room. Two women with cropped gray hair stood with their guidebooks, staring out at the sights; trucks, cars, gas pumps. The cloying sweetness of their cologne mixed with the uriney smell of the hallway. Fumes of disinfectant seeped down his throat and up toward his nose. Way stations, travel stops, scenic areas, places where no one ever stayed for longer than they could help it—why did they always smell the same? They were all marooned here on this island of gasoline, rest rooms, and fast food, all on their way somewhere else. The calming image of Northwood and the past faded into the cracked green paint and the graffiti on the urinal wall. DONNA H. IS A GREAT LAY. RICHIE SEPTEMBER 76. TOMORROW IS THE FIRST DAY OF THE REST OF YOUR LIFE. Underneath this, someone had scrawled the insipid round cartoon smile that meant "Have a Nice Day."

From an outside telephone booth opposite the auto-supply shop near the gas pumps, he called Julia. Through the plate glass he could see stacks of oil cans, and rubber fan belts hanging from pegs on the wall. A man wearing sunglasses was buying a rearview mirror from the display of chrome under the glass countertop. The telephone rang at Northwood. The man scrutinized himself in the small reflection of one of the mirrors as he held it up to his face. The mirror reflected back the image of the man's hands holding a mirror as it faced the reflecting surface of his sunglasses.

"Hi, Julie."

"Where are you?"

"I got held up in construction," he said. "There was a bad truck accident near Sturbridge. I'm about to get onto Route 93."

"You'll be here in about two hours, then?"

"Whatever, there's a bit of traffic. I hope you weren't expecting me for lunch."

"I just want to know when you're getting here," she said. He imagined her standing by the telephone in the kitchen at Northwood. He imagined the lunch table set for two, with silverware and wine glasses.

"I'll be there as soon as I can," he said.

He let the weight of his foot shift down onto the accelerator until the speedometer registered seventy-five. His instep was beginning to cramp, as it did on long trips, but he would have to speed to make up for the hour he had lied about. Route 93 was still miles down the Mass. Turnpike and after the long stretch on Route 290 through Worcester. He eyed each overpass and thicket for concealed police cars as he passed, and watched the opposite lane for the headlights-flashing warning signal that motorists sometimes give each other when they've passed a speed trap. His eyes were straining toward a likely intersection about a half mile ahead when lights started to flash in the rearview mirror. Magically materializing from nowhere, a state-police car pulled him off the road with sirens wailing. As he braked on the gravelly shoulder, he tried to remember where he had put his license. Was the registration kept in the glove compartment? The trooper looked stonily down from under the brim of his wide hat as Billy frantically rooted through the pile of maps and papers. His sweating fingers smudged the ink on his signature as he handed it over.

"Yes, sir, no sir, I'm terribly sorry, sir." Billy squirmed abjectly under the man's reproving stare.

The policeman examined the papers with distaste, like a surgeon looking at the x rays of a lung-cancer patient. "You were clocked at twenty miles over the speed limit," he said. He made this sound like the worst offense possible.

"I'm sorry, sir."

"We have too many accidents caused by speeding for me to let you off."

"Yes sir. I wouldn't expect that, sir."

"It's a serious violation. In another state you might have lost your license for this." His voice made it clear that he wished Massachusetts was one of those states.

"Yes sir. I understand, sir."

"You'll receive a summons in the mail. Is this your correct address?"

"Yes sir. Thank you, sir." Meaning fuck you, sir. Billy drove away very slowly, with adolescent rage simmering in his humiliated soul. God damn the sanctimonious bastard. What a way to start a vacation. God damn Julia and her pathetic little voice on the telephone. It was her fault he had had to lie to her, her fault that he was speeding. If it weren't for her waiting for him, he could have had a nice leisurely drive and maybe stopped for lunch somewhere off the road, instead of at that grimy Howard Johnson's.

As 290 lifted up over Worcester past the big stadium below Holy Cross, he imagined himself in the high-beamed dining room of a Connecticut country inn, the newspaper beside him as he drank a cup of steaming coffee, a basket of sweet blueberry muffins wrapped in a soft linen napkin alongside. The dining room he imagined was almost empty, but from the corner near the window a pretty woman kept glancing in his direction as she ate. He had seen her folding her long legs out of a red convertible sports car outside in the parking lot. Her interest was unmistakable. As the meal went on, she looked over more and more, and when he stood up to leave, her wide gray eyes met his directly.

His heartbeat settled back to normal as he turned off Route 495 and down under the bridge to Route 93 toward Nashua. This was the last leg, and in a minute he would be out of Massachusetts. As he drove dead north through the flat piny plains of New Hampshire, his fantasy woman slid into the seat beside him smiling. Her thick dark hair fell in soft wings on either side of her forehead. A half-unbuttoned, man-tailored silk shirt showed off her curves. She had a soft low voice with a faint English accent, and she laughed as he told her about his speeding ticket, his marriage, his job in New York. She knew that these things were unimportant. She understood that he was different from other men. He was special and powerful, a man set apart for more important things. She didn't need him or depend on him, this wonderful girl he had met by chance. She wanted him for himself. There would be no promises, only enjoyment. Real selfishness is not taking advantage of your life, she was saying. A man like you! It was wrong to stay with Julia out of a sense of obligation. Wrong to let Walter Sachs push him around. There were much greater things in store for him. With a surge of confidence, Billy stepped on the accelerator. His heart was flying. She was right! He should have a sports car instead of this dumpy little car. A convertible for sailing through the spring air with his hair pulled back in the wind. He was king of the road, he was cool, in control, the asphalt knelt down before the irresistible force of his authority.

Behind him the wail of a police siren rose above the quickening sound of tires on the roadway. Billy cursed as he steered the car onto the shoulder in front of the trooper's flashing lights.

Chapter 12

"Two speeding tickets! Do you think they'll take away your license?" Julia was waving the white slips of paper in the air over the table in the living room at Northwood.

"I hope not." He took another swallow of Scotch from the glass on the end table next to the green couch. Through the windowpanes he could see the afternoon sky darkening behind the mountain peaks on the other side of the lake. "I think I'll take a walk before dinner," he said.

"I guess I'd just have to drive you everywhere, wouldn't I? Wait a minute, I'll go with you."

He had imagined his first walk down the pasture toward the lake, alone. His lungs would fill with the transparent mountain air. His crowded mind would be soothed by the emptiness of the abandoned stables and menagerie buildings. It would be very quiet.

"Want a cracker?" She pushed a plate of saltines covered with cheese between his eyes and the view. He took one, and the gluey yellow spread seemed to lodge in his esophagus and fan out into his lungs. His breathing was choked and rapid as he stood up and walked obediently behind her to the front door.

Outside, the air seemed peculiarly thin and unsustaining. He pursed his lips together and bent over slightly, to take the pressure off his chest and push oxygen down into his bronchial tubes. As a child, these attacks had immobilized him for days. His whole body would heave and his breath would make terrifying rasping and whistling sounds as he struggled to draw air into his blocked system. When his parents leaned over him in concern, he felt as if he would suffocate. When they left the room, he knew that he had been abandoned to die alone. Now the walk downhill seemed to aggravate his problem. The air teemed with pollen. Every inhale was an effort, and he closed his mouth to suppress the sound of his wheezing.

"Are you having an asthma attack?"

"No. It's just the difference in the air." Shortness of breath kept him from a longer, more convincing disclaimer.

"Are you sure you shouldn't go back and lie down? You sound terrible. Remember, Cece had that professor who died of emphysema." Billy thought of the creaky antique beds at Northwood with their dusty pillows and deep feather comforters covered in aging fabric from Fortuny. Everything indoors was old, old and coated with the fine invisible dust of age and memories that filtered into his breathing and clogged his lungs.

"I think it's better to stay outdoors."

"Did you bring your pills?"

Instead of answering, he walked ahead of her down the hill. The pills stopped his asthma, but they made his head ache and his heart race. When they reached the old flower bed between the stables and the menagerie building, he stepped into the wide door of the barn that had been remodeled for Charley's animals. As he walked through the sliding wooden doors into the cool interior hallway his lungs seemed to ease. No people had lived out their lives in this building, the walls had no freight of human suffering, the floors didn't stink of human futility. There were no ghosts. Deep in his chest the fine threads of his capillaries released their grip on the larger veins and arteries. The rigid fleshy walls of his lung cavity relaxed. Under his shirt buttons the many-fingered tubes of his bronchi expanded slightly, allowing air to gush in toward his diaphragm.

"I feel better," he said.

"You have to be careful."

"I *am* careful."

"I just meant it might get worse as you get older." There was something unfamiliar in Julia's voice, or else it was something he had never noticed before. She almost sounded pleased at the prospect of his getting sicker.

A long hall ran the length of the building facing the five cages, which rose on the right from a cement platform bisected by a drainage ditch. Round iron bars were sunk into the concrete, close together in the monkey and lion cages and about a foot apart in the big cage for the elephant who had never arrived. In front of the bars along the hall the great iron grille threw a tracery of curving shadows. Giuseppe's whimsical iron monkeys crouched in the laurel on the middle cage, and a stately wrought-iron pachyderm was cleverly woven into a frieze of laurel, ivy and palm trees in front of the elephant cage. The background design in the grille, the graceful tangle of laurel and ivy curving back on each other, was repeated in iron grilles set into the concrete floor for heating and drainage ducts.

Darwin Gibbs had once given Billy a tour of the underground cellar of the building, pointing with quiet pride to the technologically advanced drainage system and the luxurious heating system. A huge wood-burning furnace dominated the cellar under the elephant cage. Darwin had explained how the furnace heat was carried up into the cage without smoke by having the whole thing encased in tin flashing, with the chimney going right out through it. The heat traveled up between the furnace and the flashing to the open floor grille. The smoke went up the chimney. The monkeys and the lions there lived more comfortably than Darwin and his family ever had. Another man might have resented it, but anything well done, especially a building or a garden, seemed to give Darwin great satisfaction regardless of its effect on his own life. He lived by a code of manners and rituals that were the more impressive for being mysterious to someone who had been brought up in the affluent suburban middle class, as Billy had. Darwin had the weasely body and narrow face of generations of New Hampshire inbreeding, but there was a shrewdness and an eagerness about him that had attracted Charley enough so that he rescued him from a job in the shoe factory in Concord and brought him to work at Northwood.

Once, when Billy had gone up to the garden to find Darwin and say good-by on the last day of summer, the bony old man in blue overalls had wheeled on his cracked boot and walked away. How have I offended him? Billy thought. Then he saw that Darwin had turned to wash the dirt off his hands in the rain barrel before coming to say his farewell. Billy had felt effete and plump and strangely blessed when the worker folded his small pale hand in his own huge dirt-encrusted fingers still damp from the wooden font of sweet water.

Darwin's wife had died the same year Charley did, and since then Northwood's caretaker seemed to have aged twenty years and lost interest in almost everything. He only came up to the place once a week now, and Billy knew he spent most of his time in the dingy living room of his farm-house, watching game shows on the television set he had bought with the money Charley left him.

The empty elephant cage was the centerpiece of the build-ing. The wide board walls and high windows gave an archi-tectural sense of New England, while the elaborate grille suggested the ancient and durable craft of ironworking that had passed from generation to generation of European arti-sans. There were no claustrophobic memories here, only the reassuring sense that the work of men had gone on for hun-dreds and thousands of years and would continue for hun-dreds and thousands more. Billy stepped through the gate in the wrought-iron grille, unlatching it by turning the key that lay in the lock at waist level, and slipped through the bars of the cage. The wheezing was gone. He thought of the slow, relaxed, ponderous movements of an elephant, the gray warmth of its wrinkled flanks, the lazy swinging of its mas-sive trunk.

"The wall is buckling, up there. See it?" Julia was pointing from the other side of the grille toward the wall over his head. Through the scrim of bars and iron she looked oddly alien to him, as if the separation marked them as different species. He turned and examined the wall. Water from the outside had leaked through the cinder block during the winter snows, and the wooden walls on the inside were pushing inward and bubbling away from the two-by-fours that held them. It would be an easy-enough job to pry the warped wood off the posts and hammer new boards into place.

"I can fix that," Billy said. He would sweat and stretch as he hammered and lifted. Then he could lie on his back on the straw pallets at the side of the cage and look up at the ironwork and daydream.

"Maybe I can get Darwin to help with the boathouse before Cece comes," she said.

"When's she coming?" Through the tracery of the grille, Billy saw a female human in a yellow blouse lift her torso and drop her neck in a shrug.

"She was supposed to be here by now," she said.

"How are your vegetables doing?" He reached out through the grille and turned the lock, pushing against the door to let himself out again. Julia had walked down to the end of the hallway, and the dimness in the building as evening fell hid her face in the shadows.

"The lettuce is up," she said. "It's hard without Darwin to help out. The boathouse is more important." Her voice came disembodied from the gloom. "We don't really need the vegetables." He thought about the boats, hoisted up in their racks at the side of the boathouse waiting out the winter snows in silence. He usually got the canoe down for the summer, but when Charley was alive there were always three or four boats out, canoes and the catboat and the mahogany Chris-Craft, floating in their slips under the boathouse. He could swim under the wall and into the watery enclosure where they were moored. The light came up under the boards at the side, reflecting off the sand in shifting patterns of yellow and green. The lake slapped gently against the keels.

"How did the cover go?" Julia's question pulled him back from his daydream as they left the building and stepped back out onto the grass. With a start he remembered his job. Even up here they would be calling him every day until the issue was finally closed and distributed. He wished they would leave him alone, but he was glad they needed him. Sometimes the bind of his own anxieties made him think about being less successful. He thought with longing of real nine-to-five jobs, the kinds of jobs where going home meant that the work was over and you didn't have to think about it until the next day. It would be nice to be a secretary, or someone's dizzy wife. Even the animals' lives seemed so easy sometimes. The lions and the monkeys, Charley's old Labrador, Sandy; they didn't have to worry about obligations and responsibilities. Everything was taken care of for them by other people, their owners. No one was after them to rewrite this or edit that or quit drinking or cut down on cholesterol. No one demanded explanations for their behavior. Peaceful and routine, their days passed in dreamy silences. He understood why paroled criminals broke the law again and again until they were finally caught so that they could go back to prison. In prison they were taken care of.

"Come on, let's get back up to the house," Julia said. "I put a bottle of that good vodka in the freezer."

He tried to anticipate the haze of good will the vodka

would bring him. Rolling saliva on his tongue, he thought about its cool taste and voluptuous texture as it slid out of the bottle into his glass. He couldn't shake his anxiety.

"Good," he said. "When do you think Cece is coming?" What if something had happened to her? What if something had gone wrong?

"Next week, I hope." As they started up the lawn toward the house, he felt her hand light on his forearm below the rolled-up sleeve of his shirt. "I'm glad you're here," she said. "I was kind of scared up here alone."

"What's for dinner?"

"I wish you would listen to me sometimes, Billy."

"I *was* listening." He stopped and turned toward her, leaning slightly forward. "You said you were glad I was here because you were kind of scared up here alone."

"Oh, never mind." She put her hands away in the pockets of her Bermuda shorts and took a step toward the house. The fieldstone foundation had already turned from gray to black with the deepening evening light. Above it the white wood glistened with the last rays of the sun.

"No really. I *am* listening. Tell me what you were scared about."

In the fading light he could see her shrug. "It was silly, I guess. I just kept thinking about all those empty rooms. Someone could have gotten in or something. I don't know."

"Oh, Julie, nothing could happen to you up here." He reached out to put a comforting hand on her shoulder. His mind imagined her bloodied, beaten body lying across one of the woven rag rugs in the third-story bedrooms. "It's a safe place."

"I know." She slumped and put her hand back on his arm. "What's the matter with me anyway?"

"Nothing, silly." In the eerie light her face looked twisted and unfamiliar.

"I just keep thinking horrible things," she said.

"Nothing's the matter with you that a nice vacation won't fix," he said. "Now stop thinking that way, we're going to have a wonderful time." He put his arm around her narrow shoulders and took a definite step toward the house.

"I guess you're right." She let out a long breath and followed his lead.

"Of *course* I'm right." He swept her along up the grass toward the shadows of the broad porch. "We're having a wonderful time. What's for dinner?"

Together they walked up the lawn, a tall man in city clothes with his arm around a balky woman in a yellow blouse. They looked oddly out of place and awkward in the untended wilderness of the landscape as night fell. Behind them the lake glowered up at the reddening sky. Ahead the house, gabled and shadowy, seemed to embrace the darkness that came down out of the woods, over the foundations of abandoned farms, across the fading mirrors of beaver ponds, and onto the unplowed fields of the upper forty. Owls hooted and badgers woke up and scrambled out of their holes and bears bumped around somewhere in the darkness. The rapidly cooling air pricked at Billy's skin as if some invisible presence was trying to hold him back. He thought of the darkness in the empty upper rooms and shivered. Behind Julia he walked up the steps into the brooding arches of the porch.

Chapter 13

I N HIS DREAM, THE BIG OLD Labrador was sitting at the top of the steps on the porch. "Sandy," he called, "Sandy come here, here Sandy." He whistled a high and then a low note. "Come on, Sandy."

The dog cocked his broad muzzle toward the sound. Then he cleared his throat with a noise that was suddenly completely human. "I'm not Sandy anymore," he said, explaining this to Billy as if Billy was a child who couldn't be expected to know any better. "I'm a man now. I'm tired of being a dog." His warm brown eyes commanded Billy's consent and understanding.

At the end, Sandy had been a lame-legged construction of

bones and graying fur, his aging pupils white with cataracts. Even Julie had stopped calling him Alexander—the name Charley thought appropriate for his hunting dog. But in the dream old Sandy had a kind of gentle authority that made his statement seem natural and easy to believe.

"I'm a man now," he said. "I'm not a dog anymore." And Billy had no choice but to nod an amazed agreement.

Its strangeness came back to him, pushing up through the details of the morning as he drove down the hill and took the right turn for Granville Center. The town was open for the flood of free-spending tourists that somehow seemed to evade it year after year. The tourist-information center was draped with ratty crepe paper, a sidewalk sign in front of Moody's Drugstore advertised fly-specked cones and sundaes, and on the outskirts Hoadley's Amusement Park and Fantastic Carnival Rides had arrived for a week on its seasonal tour of busted New England towns. The Ferris wheel jerked in its orbit with two children screaming and giggling in the highest seat. Their parents watched through the windshield of their car. The woman was eating a doughnut.

Billy was glad not to have to wait in traffic for a parking space on the green, or bribe the drugstore clerk to save a newspaper for him, or scheme to get the services of a plumber or an electrician the way summer people did in the popular vacation towns like North Conway and Peterborough. Still, annual failure and the grind of poverty gave Granville Center a bleakness that made him avoid trips into the town if he could. People on the streets were taciturn, their faces numb with trouble, their thoughts locked inside where they considered how to make frayed ends meet.

He pulled up to the curb next to the lumberyard, and walked through the racks of planks and rods toward the tearing scream of the electric saw at the back. Franklin Cavis came forward from the shed to shake his hand; Cavis's son continued to feed boards into the saw without looking up. The noise obliterated conversation.

"I'll need about five of these boards," Billy said, laying one hand on the splintery surface of a stack of cut pine near the door and holding up five fingers with his other hand.

Franklin nodded. Decades of intermarriage and inbreeding had left their stamp on Granville Center; there were two or three principal bloodlines, and almost all the natives were clearly identifiable by build and feature as belonging to one or another of Granville Center's oldest families. The Gibbses were wiry and sharp-featured. The Cavises were broad-faced and beefy. As Franklin nodded, his wide cheeks that looked as if they had been built for a smile remained implacably still. His eyes were hidden by the smeared lenses of his wire-rimmed glasses, and a grimy International Harvester cap threw a visor's shadow across his face. Huge hands grabbed the five boards on the top of the pile and lifted them up to rest on Cavis's broad shoulder. Billy followed him out to the car.

On the sidewalk two stray tourists stood and gazed through the window of Moody's: a fat man in blue pants that stretched grotesquely over his thighs, and a girl with frizzy hair and an orange T-shirt. POLISH T-SHIRT, the lettering on the front of the T-shirt said. It was printed upside down. As Franklin Cavis loaded the boards into the back of the station wagon, Billy watched the man in the stretch pants decide against Moody's and climb back into the white car they had parked at the curb. Massachusetts plates, they probably got lost, he thought. The man reached into a Dunkin' Donuts box and extricated a lump of greasy cake as they passed Billy on their way out of town.

As he drove past Gillingham's Hardware Store and the Woolworth five-and-ten, Billy noticed that a new Fourth of July banner had been added to the front of the Granville Tap Room. Underneath it a grizzled farmer in overalls sat on the steps hefting a Narragansett beer can. Billy turned left and rounded the village green, a placid patch of ground ringed with the kind of maple-shaded white frame houses with green shutters that you see on postcards of picturesque New England. The center of the green was usurped by a large cannon mounted on a concrete slab, and a memorial to the Granville Center dead. The boards rattled in the back of the car as he turned off the asphalt onto the steep dirt road to Northwood.

Julia came out on the front porch as he was unloading the boards. The screen door slammed behind her. "Your office called. I said you'd call them back," she said.

He pulled the boards out of the car over the tailgate and hoisted them onto his shoulder. Cavis had lifted them effortlessly. Their unwieldy weight bent Billy's body and pulled an ache into his lower back. He steadied them in their precarious position and started down the hill.

"Why does she have to call you here? Don't they know you're on vacation?" Her voice sounded an octave higher.

"Of course she knows." As he passed the porch the wood started to cut into the back of his neck, a sharp pain spread across his shoulders. If he could just keep moving, he could get the boards down to the menagerie building in one load. If he had to stop, the burden would overwhelm him. Staggering slightly, he continued down the hill.

"Well, why does she call, then?"

The five slats began to slide apart as he passed the old flower border. If he speeded up his steps, he still might make it.

"Are you going to answer me or not?"

He let the boards drop. They banged against his shoulder and clattered to the ground at his feet. A sharp splinter throbbed in his wrist.

"Sherry calls me because she is my secretary." He spoke slowly and deliberately to keep himself from exploding. "She is only doing her job. They have to reach me here because there are still decisions to be made while the cover closes."

"They couldn't do that without you?"

"Of course they could." He bent over to pick up the boards. Now he would have to lift them two at a time; it would take three trips to get them down to the menagerie. "I'm sorry it bothers you so much," he said. "I need to talk to them because I care enough about my work so that it's important to me to get even the trivial last-minute things done well." The idea that they might have gone ahead and closed his story without him, expressed in Julia's high whine, made him feel nauseous. He didn't want them to do it without him. If they did too many things without him, soon enough they would realize they could do everything without him. Like they had realized about Frank Cushing.

"At least you admit you *want* them to call you here," Julia said. "I never heard *that* before." She turned with a shrug and went back through the screen door. It slammed behind her.

It was a hot day, but inside the menagerie the earth was cool and the air smelled of straw and wood. Billy lay on his back on the animal pallets, breathing hard from the job of carrying the boards down and stacking them next to the wall. The eerie silence of the building seemed to spread out for miles. In the distance he could hear the faint buzz of a motorboat somewhere on the lake and the low pleasing hum of a car speeding by on the highway at the bottom of the hill. The light from the high windows came in through the grillework, casting grotesque shadows on the hammer and plane and wrecking bar waiting for him to go to work. If he just lay there, things would get better. Julia would calm down after the cover was out. Cece would come. Soon his worst problem would be deciding whether to drive into Concord to buy the magazine or whether to leave well enough alone.

He hated himself for caring so much about the way they played his stories. Would they put his by-line at the top, or in a string of them at the end? Would he rate a mention in the table of contents? What did he care? He shifted position and pushed against the pallet to feel the satisfying scratch and tickle of the hay through the fabric of his polo shirt. Charley North had wanted an elephant to live here. Now it was his son-in-law who lay sprawled on the straw. Men had dreamed before and been disappointed before. Life would go on, elephant or no elephant, magazine or no magazine, marriage or no marriage.

With the wrecking bar he pried the first of the warped boards away from the beams that were bolted to the concrete outer wall. The nails came out with a metallic shrieking sound. He pulled against the wood gently, to keep it from splintering. If the boards broke off it would be harder to get the nails out. Holding one of the new boards up to the empty space on the wall, he saw that it fit very well. Things were better already. With the claw end of the hammer, he hooked onto each nailhead and pulled, yanking it out of the beams in a long curve.

The highest boards were out of his reach, and he would have to find a ladder in one of the sheds. Resting it on the cement would be tricky, though; in the floor against the back wall was a manhole-sized iron grille from the heating duct, which led to the furnace in the basement below. Charley had hated the smell of burning coal, and so even in the menagerie all the furnaces burned wood. A staff of four had stoked them three times a day when it was cold, from mountains of logs and kindling stacked in the cellar. Twice a year great truckloads of wood had been delivered to Northwood, and burly men in the trucks would jump out and unload into the chute to the cellar, with Darwin supervising the whole operation.

The rhythm of manual work absorbed Billy. Pry, pull, hook, pry, pull, hook. If he kept at it steadily, a big piece of the old siding would be off before lunch. The wood came away with a satisfying crackling sound. The old nails clinked as they dropped to the concrete floor and rolled away from the heating ducts. He could call the office in the afternoon when Julia was up in the garden.

"Billy?" Her voice behind him startled him into an involuntary jump.

"You surprised me," he said. As he turned, he saw her watching him from the other side of the bars and grillework. All that wild iron had the effect of giving her a surreal quality, as if she were a woman in a picture, or an example of an endangered breed living out her life in captivity.

"I'm sorry I was so cranky before," she said, leaning her face against the grille. "Lunch is ready."

"This is going to be a bigger job than I thought," he said.

"Sometimes I just get so nervous about everything."

"Well, I've started at least. See how much of the siding is off already?" He collected his tools and propped them against the wall under the boards.

"I know how silly it is," she said.

"Don't worry about it, Julie, we all get nervous sometimes," he said. "I may need some new nails. I wonder if there are any in the tool shed."

He walked across the elephant cage toward her, turning his body sideways to slip through the iron bars inside of the door in the grille. Reaching out with his palm, he pushed gently against the metal doorjamb to open it. Nothing happened. He reached out and grabbed a clump of the ornamental ivy and pushed harder, rattling iron against iron. It was stuck. With a strong shove he pushed his shoulder against the door. It still didn't move.

"I guess I must have locked myself in," he said. "Stupid." The key jutted from the iron lock on the outside of the grille. Billy reached through the curves of ivy, turned the lock, and let himself out, leaving the key in the latch as he curved his hand back around the doorway.

"Can you believe I did that?"

Julia was already halfway out of the building. He closed the gate behind him and followed her up to the house.

Chapter 14

IT WAS STILL EARLY MORNING. As Julia turned over the soil in the vegetable garden, night cold came steaming out into the sunlight. The string beans that Darwin had planted were up, and there were already tiny heads of buttercrunch and kale, enough for a salad at lunchtime. The corn hills were done, and the long blades of grass pushed out of the mounds of earth—blades of grass that would dominate the garden with great stalks and tassels. Julia moved from row to row, propping up the tomato plants and weeding the broccoli. Her triumph this year was the strawberry bed at the south end of the plot. Ten plants spread their deep-green runners out over the dark earth, and she knelt down to

pick the seedy ripe berries from under the leaves. Next to
them, at the end of the garden, she could see that the fence
was rusted and torn, but it seemed to be keeping the animals
out so far.

The fence itself was nailed to one of the gigantic white
wooden posts still standing where the gate to the original
garden had once been. Now there was no gate, only these
two columns, like the remnants of Ozymandias' kingdom,
with a chicken-wire fence nailed against them. In the old
days, Northwood had had a ten-acre vegetable garden and
two smaller flower gardens down near where she could see
the wreckage of the greenhouses. The whole place had been
a patchwork of color, landscaped around rock gardens and
rosebushes, with borders along all the paths and nasturtium
and alyssum beds along the front of the house. All that had
grown over now, and was barely discernible as slightly ragged places in the grass. Like a dying lake, the garden had receded to this pathetic corner of earth.

She piled the soil into little hills and used a trowel to
scoop out ditches for the tomato plants she had bought in the
village. The seedlings were damp, and each one kept the
configuration of its papier-mâché pot as she tenderly put it in
the ground, tamping the earth around its roots with her fingers. Now they were delicate and a frost would kill them. By
September they would be robust vines breaking under the
weight of the red globes she always took back to New York
by the bushel to give away. The earth was so wonderfully
reliable. Each year it worked the same magic, as seeds she
could barely see to plant sprang out of their shells and into a
hearty rampage of vegetables and flowers. The garden was
comfortingly neat and predictable. Here, at least, the malevolent forces of nature were on her side for a moment. The

dew on the fresh green leaves seemed to wink at her. She bent down again to the strawberry plants to fill her quart basket. With her free hand she dipped one of the berries into the rain barrel and popped it in her mouth, where it exploded with the sweet tart taste of summer days.

She could hear the telephone ringing in the house. Ten o'clock, it was probably Billy's secretary Sherry again. After two rings, the sound stopped. She would not notice how long he took on the telephone. She would not look at her watch and then check it again when she finally heard the slam of the screen door that meant he had gone down to the menagerie building. She did not care. The garden sustained her. Seventeen minutes.

In town, Julia parked the station wagon in front of Gillingham's and consulted her shopping list. Hardware store, Granville Market, Woolworth's for some string to tie the tomato plants to the fence. Spaghetti for dinner. Frozen vegetables and a salad made of the leaves of her own lettuce from the garden. In Gillingham's she paced back and forth in the tool section looking for a smaller cultivator. Mr. Gillingham used to come out of the back room or step from behind the cash register every time Julia and her parents came into the store. He wore a white smock and a straw boater that he would hold in front of his heart as he stopped to chat and to help them find whatever they needed in the indecipherable maze of tools and paper products and nails and crackers and magazines. The turkey on the table at Eighty-first Street at Christmastime had always been sent down from one of Mr. Gillingham's food lockers, and when Julia was a little girl there was a lollipop for her in a special hiding place behind the counter. Now Mr. Gillingham was dead, and his family had had to sell the store. Julia gave her money to a surly young man with a swelling pimple on his lip and a greasy pompadour of black hair.

Granville Center still looked as picturesque as it had then. No swarms of tourists crowded the curbs, no tacky boutiques of phony "native craft" shops had intruded on the façade along Main Street, no rows of cheap summer bungalows lined the lakefront. When she heard about scenic New England, Julia always thought of little Granville Center, with its eighteenth-century houses clustered around the green and the maples in summer leaf.

As she walked past the war memorial, she remembered her parents and the way they stood out at the dedication ceremony the town had held there thirty years ago. They were clearly and fashionably apart from the gray inbred townspeople. Her father wore a double-breasted white linen suit, the one he called his ice-cream suit, and her mother wore a silk dress and a round hat with a curve of gray feathers over the back of it. But they were welcome there anyway. Mr. and Mrs. North don't you know they have a big summer place down the lake Darwin Gibbs works up there say hello to them Edith. And Charley would bow to the men and take off his custom-made straw fedora for the ladies. Everybody loved Charley North.

She crossed the street in front of the courthouse and the town hall on her way back to the car. Her father used to say that there was more of a town hall in Granville Center than there was a town. It was a squat brick building with mullioned windows and arched portals that local historians claimed had been designed by H. H. Richardson in the great New England tradition of Richardson town halls and libraries. One of the windows had been broken and replaced with plywood, and the bricks at the edge of the arches seemed to be crumbling. The clock that dominated the façade was permanently stopped.

"The town hall really needs some restoration," she said to Billy over dinner.

"The whole town could use some work." He helped himself to more spaghetti sauce.

"I wonder if it really is a Richardson building?"

"I doubt it." Minute polka dots of tomato sauce were already speckled across his shirt front.

"Why don't you tuck your napkin into your shirt when we have spaghetti, dear?" Tomorrow she would do a wash. The dryer was broken. If the sun came out she could hang the clothes on the line.

"Oh, damn! I always get this bloody sauce on my shirt." Billy stood up from the table and walked into the kitchen leaving the dinner she had cooked for him less than half eaten.

"Never mind, I'll do a wash tomorrow," she called through the doorway. "Come and eat." She could see him angrily rubbing at his shirt front with the dishwashing sponge. "Why don't you leave it?"

"Is it better to use cold water on this, or soap?" his voice came back from the kithcen. "I can't seem to get it out."

Leaving her own dinner, she walked into the kitchen. The front of his shirt was covered with soaking wet blotches, some still sticking to the pink surface of skin underneath. The tiny dots of tomato sauce had become long jagged stains.

"Here, let me do it." He stood passively and allowed her to rub the sauce out with warm water and soap. As she worked, inches from his heart, Julia was suddenly overtaken by a gust of absolute rage. He was so helpless! So pathetic! When Billy tried to do anything he always had to ask her how so many times that it was easier to do it herself. He got himself into trouble, stubbornly refused to listen to her advice, and then expected her to rescue him. Rubbing away at his shirt, a shirt she had bought, laundered, and mended without thanks, she was angry enough to kill him. The carving knife. The frying pan. But what she felt like doing was throttling him, shaking him, letting her anger out at him until he died. He was so stupid he just stood there.

"That'll do it," she said. "The rest will come out in the wash." She focused on the back of his neck as he walked back to the dining-room table. One swift chop in that vulnerable downy spot. When she got back to the table the spaghetti sauce was cold. Oil was congealing around the edges of her plate.

"I always spill spaghetti sauce." Billy sat firmly back in his chair, glaring at the white starch string tangles with personal animosity. It was her fault for serving spaghetti. She knew he always spilled the sauce.

"Salad?" She tossed the fresh leaves in the big hardwood bowl, coating them with a shimmering film of dressing. "It looks good."

"No thanks."

"It's fresh lettuce from the garden."

"I just can't figure out why I always spill it like that. I never spill anything else."

As she lifted the glistening leaves of lettuce onto her plate, she concentrated on thinking about the garden. Even now, at this very moment, the vegetables and strawberries were out there in the darkness growing in their symmetrical patterns, blooming and ripening. The predictable unchanging progress of each plant's growth was something apart from her own anger and her own feelings and Billy's stupidity. It would go on no matter what they did, as plants had sprouted and grown always. The leaves tasted like the morning air.

Chapter 15

JULIA LAY AWAKE STARING OUT AT the beginning of the summer day. It was Wednesday. Going-to-the-dump day. The birches at the edge of the meadow already cast their lissome shadows on the high alfalfa and hay. Birds began to chirp in the oak trees outside the house. By turning over and looking out the north window, she could see uphill into the woods where the soft shadows of tree trunks shed a mysterious singing light over the ferns and moss at their roots. The jumble of her dreams, where a train roared through landscapes and her mother was sitting in the living room talking about Labradors, had been shattered by a contraction of anxiety. Something was going wrong. But now the morning gently washed the birches with pale gold light.

"Are you awake?" she whispered at Billy's inert back.

His answer was a muttered snore. She held the carved bedpost for balance and swung her legs over the side of the four-poster. The wooden floor was cool underfoot; the tiles in the bathroom icy. She hopped over them to the bathmat and turned the cold-water faucet on. As toothpaste squirted onto her brush, she caught her reflection in the mirror. The dim gold- and silver-speckled surface showed her the face of a very pretty woman. But she knew the lines and wrinkles that the old mirror didn't show. Even her cheeks below the puckery surface at the side of her eyes were beginning to collapse, as if the bones underneath were slowly dissolving. Crow's-feet were from smiling, they said, and the lines at the edge of the mouth were from talking, and the vertical lines above her upper lip were from smoking, and the deep creases in the forehead were from quizzical expressions, and the two indentations along the top of her nose were from frowns. There was no worst spot, no one thing to have tucked or lifted by the nimble hands of a society surgeon. The whole thing was a simultaneous disaster, especially the lines in her cheeks, which she could see if she looked hard enough, even in this dark glass. She puffed her face out with air, and they disappeared. She relaxed and they appeared again. Quickly she bent her head over the sink and sawed hard at her teeth and gums with the toothbrush. There was blood in the mixture of peppermint and water when she spat back into the basin.

* * *

"If you're going to the dump," Billy said over breakfast, "why don't you take that broken plant stand? It's just cluttering up the tool shed."

"You don't think it could be fixed?"

"Are you kidding? Pass the muffins, please."

"Mrs. Cavis baked these," she said, handing him the breadbasket with its linen napkin folded over brown lumps of warm dough. "Do you want to come up to the garden this morning? The fence needs some work."

"It figures," he said. "They taste like sawdust."

"You have other plans?"

"Look at this." He rattled the pages of the *Manchester Union Leader* and folded them lengthwise. "Here's a wire-service story on corporate alcoholism and how big business is handling it."

"What are you going to do this morning?"

"I bet they took it right out of my cover. Some bastard must have sneaked them an early copy."

"What are you going to do this morning?" She raised her voice slightly this time.

"Hmmm?" His head popped up from the paper as if he had heard her question for the first time. "Oh. I guess I'd better call the office first," he said. "Then I'll go down and work on that wall."

Leaving Billy hidden behind the newspaper, she dropped the trowel and cultivator into her gardening basket and started down the driveway. Later she would get the mail and make his lunch and go to the dump, if she had time. In the old days, Northwood had had its own dump, a stone-lined pit at the end of a dirt road that was now an overgrown track in the meadow. Darwin would load up the truck and rumble down the road with the day's worth of compost and garbage.

At the end of the summer they would burn the accumulation, and the flames and smoke would go so high you could see them from the top of Tenney Mountain five miles away. The Granville Center Fire Department had had to give them a special permit, and the village fire truck with the hook and ladder would come and park in the driveway while the fire burned. Cook gave them pitchers of fruit punch and home-made butter cookies.

Now the dump was a big boxy cement building with an incinerator out near Meredith, and the air all around it had the same hard smell of cinders that belched out of chimneys in New York City. The garbage had to be separated into bottles and cans and degradables before they would even accept it. The men worked in stained green coveralls, and they never smiled. The road into the building was lined with smoldering heaps of ash and rubble stretching up to the top of the hill and as far north as you could see. Old cast-iron beds and bits of wood stuck up out of the debris. She probably wouldn't have time to go to the dump.

The driveway continued down a slight grade to the road, and where the path to the garden broke away up the hill a great balsam stood. Its spiky bunches of needles blocked out the sun, and on the lowest of its huge perpendicular branches she could see the two bolts that had been the anchor for Cece's swing, and for her swing before that. She passed the balsam and started toward the gates. The beans would be higher this morning. There would be fresh leaves unfurling from the tight yellow lettuce buds, and more ripe strawberries. Every day there were changes. But as she got closer, Julia could see that the neat rows of vegetables were somehow distorted. Something had gone wrong.

Each tender lettuce plant had been jaggedly sawed off at

root level. The tomato vines had been torn from their supports and trampled into the dirt. The green beans were uprooted and scattered all over what was left of the broccoli. The corn hills were gone, a few gnawed stubs of their roots were the only remnant. Beanpoles lay like bars over the broken plants. Julia remembered the splintered wood and awkward angles of her mother's ruined plant stand. She remembered the burst cushions and exploded viscera of the old sofa at home. The fence had not kept the animals out after all.

She stepped inside the fence, still hoping that her vision would evaporate, restoring the neat rows and fruitful earth of yesterday. Nature was malevolent. When she forgot that even for a moment, nature punished her. Only the strawberry bed had miraculously escaped the invasion of deer or woodchucks. They must have been frightened by something. She leaned over and picked one of the red hearts off the vine. That was all they had left her.

She walked numbly back down to the house. As she passed above the menagerie building she could hear the sound of hammering, Billy nailing the new boards to their wooden supports. There was no point in replanting the garden now. It was too late to begin corn or green beans or tomatoes. Lettuce would take two weeks to come up. In the kitchen she stared blankly at the breakfast dishes. Rinse and stack. No knives in the dishwasher. Two spoonfuls of grainy blue soap go in the container on the door. The rhythmic pound of the machine as it washed seemed to find an echo in her temples. She stepped out on the porch.

From the menagerie building the sound of hammering alternated with the groaning of old boards being pulled off the walls. Sometimes there were long periods of silence. Daydreaming, probably. Oh God! Why had she ended up married to a man who was always in such a fog? It wasn't even worth trying to get through to him about what had happened to the garden. He wouldn't understand. He would think she was blaming him for not mending the fence. If he thought anything at all. Half the time she felt as if she were talking to a brick wall, a husband dummy, a person who wasn't there. "Oh, that's too bad, sweetie," he would say if she told him about it at lunch. "I guess we'll have to buy vegetables now *(munch, munch)*. Was there any interesting mail?" She hoped that at least he was that vague with everyone, and not just her. As long as he was working in the menagerie she knew where he was. Not gossiping with his slutty secretary on the telephone. Not strutting around Granville Center letting other women be taken in by that absent, vulnerable look in his handsome eyes.

The mailbox stood next to the storm gutters where the steep driveway up to Northwood joined the straight flat asphalt of the road into town. The small heap of mail inside was dwarfed by the huge green metal box left over from the days when Charley got dozens of letters and packages every day even in the summer. There was a bill from New Hampshire Light and Power. A flier from the First National in Meredith. Pork chops were down to $1.25 a pound. And two letters, one from Cece and one for Billy from his office. She slit open the envelope from her daughter with its Berkeley postmark. It was written on the monogrammed notepaper that Julia had given her last Christmas. Since this gesture was meant to please her, the letter obviously would not. Why couldn't she have called at least? Julia asked silently as she tore open the heavy flap and pulled out the slip of vellum lined in pale gray.

"Dear Mummy and Daddy." The letter was written in the round backhanded script Cece had learned at Ash Hill Country Day. "I hope you are having a nice summer. I miss you both. I know you will be disappointed, but I am very, very happy." A trailer truck swished by on the highway, its backdraft pushing Julia toward the woods. "Right off I had better say that I can't come to Northwood this summer," the letter went on. Cece had turned the page here, so that her brief message would appear to take up both sides of the notepaper. "But the reason is that Jerry and I are going to drive to Las Vegas next week and get married. I'm sorry there won't be a big wedding like you planned sometimes, Mummy, but this is what Jerry wants. I'll really miss seeing you and the old place but I hope you can come to California and visit us soon. All I can say is that I am so happy right now that it's hard to believe anyone else could be unhappy. Jerry is the right husband for me—I know it, and after all these bad times he has come around to agreeing with me I guess. Oh Mummy, do you know what it's like to be loved? Nobody ever told me I could fly like this and it makes me love both of you more. Lots of hugs and kisses . . ." Another truck passed. The driver honked at Julia, and the harsh sound echoed down the valley.

She leaned her forehead against the hot metal roof of the car and let the letter drop through the open window onto the front seat. Damn Cece and her irresponsibility! Somehow Julia had known she wasn't coming. Even as she spent time and money redecorating her bedroom, even as she planned to clean the upstairs for her arrival at Northwood. Cece had always been inconsiderate. But this was worse, even worse than she had expected. Her daughter was sneaking off for a quickie wedding with a man they had never met. She was probably pregnant, for Christ's sake. Otherwise what would make them rush to some tacky neon chapel in Las Vegas, when they could have had a beautiful wedding with the family at St. James in Ash Hill? Julia pushed her forehead against the metal roof and gripped the sharp edge of the window. How was she supposed to explain this betrayal to Billy? It was typical of his darling daughter to leave the dirty work to her mother. Would they have to pretend they were happy about Cece getting married this way? *Her* father would have flown out there and gotten the girl and brought her right back home as soon as he got the letter. But Charley North was dead.

Oh Mummy do you know what it's like to be loved? Charley could have shown her that if she knew anything about love she wouldn't be behaving this way. Julia had raised the girl. Worked and schemed to get her a good education and see that she knew what to wear and how to behave. Billy had adored Cece so much that he could never discipline her. The hard work had been left up to her mother. Do you know what it's like to be loved! She imagined Jerry and Cece walking arm in arm on the promenade at Fort Point under the Golden Gate Bridge in the sunset. He was tall and dark and leaned down to catch her every word. Cece's body was firm and smooth, as if her skin fit perfectly over the bones and muscles just beneath it. Her cheeks were taut and her eyelids unpuffy. When she smiled, her face didn't collapse into creases. Jerry loved Cece and Billy loved Cece.

Now that she had raised her daughter, her usefulness was passed. Her looks were gone. Her father who had loved *her* was dead. She was nobody's daughter and nobody's mother and nobody's special girl. Beyond the car the trees seemed to fall away in front of her eyes like the odd slipping of the landscape when a train begins to move away from the station. If she relaxed, she would sink. And who cared! Later when Billy left her for another woman they would laugh about her, and Jerry and Cece would join them. Two couples in love. A man could always find a younger woman. Acid seemed to be burning holes in her stomach, a raw feeling seeped upward into her throat.

The second letter was from Billy's office. She had never opened his mail before, but now she slit open the long business envelope with her fingernail. If he was having an affair, she might as well know it. She pulled the sheet of paper clear, and flattened it out against the hood. A car passed close enough so that its backdraft sent the dirt on the shoulder of the road swirling around her bare legs and into her sandals. Its honking wailed back at her as it sped ahead down the valley.

The letter was a list of captions for the alcoholism cover, or at least that was what it looked like.

Corporate concerns: Executives in ITT's rehabilitation program.

"It's hard to admit it to yourself": Betty Ford addresses a meeting of Alcoholics Anonymous.

High Spirits: Canadian Club's macho advertising.

Underneath this, a handwritten note in spidery black script filled the rest of the page:

"As per phoner forwarding caption blues. The terminals went down so expect more proofs tomorrow. That creepy old Ben McKay is pinching for you. Miss you already. Love, S.''

They even had a secret language! An indecipherable code that she, Billy's legal wife, could hardly understand. And "Love, S"! What else could that possibly mean? Sour fluid filled her mouth, and a stomach pain forced her over onto her elbows on the hood.

"Does she read your mail up there? I tried to be careful." Sherry was sitting in Billy's office chair. In his lap. She kissed his neck.

"That feels good," he said.

"She's so nosy! Do you want to go back to my apartment after lunch?"

"Mmmm, you know I do." Billy's eyes were closed, his face ecstatic with satisfaction.

Julia imagined Billy leaning forward to focus on Sherry at lunch as she talked across the table. He heard every word. He answered her questions. In bed, he was on top of her, his fingers laced into hers with an urgency he had lost with his own wife years ago.

It had to be true. With the certainty that he was unfaithful came a rush of longing for him. The years of devotion. The trials of bringing up his child. The perfectly planned meals and the drives to the railroad station over icy roads had all been worth it. But she knew that if she confronted him with this, he would be forced to acknowledge the truth. The truth was that he didn't care about her anymore. Then their marriage would be over. She let her full weight rest against the scorching steel of the car and tried to keep from sobbing. Tears splashed onto the shiny green surface. Her heart felt like a stone that might tear right down through her body of its own hard weight. She folded the letter back in its envelope and got into the car. Her hand turned the ignition key and pushed the gearshift into Drive. With the letters on the seat beside her, she drove up the hill. It was lunchtime.

"Do you want to come up to the house for lunch? I brought down a beer and some sandwiches." His back was turned to her in the half-light as he single-mindedly hammered a nail into a board against the opposite wall of the cage. For a moment she had imagined him turning toward her with love in his eyes. Love that turned to concern as he saw how upset she was. Concern that turned to comforting and reassurance as she spilled out all her discoveries and suspicions and fears. She would break down against his broad chest, crying to release the deep sorrow that had hold of her, and he would hug her and soothe her.

"Hey, Billy, here's some lunch," she tried again, louder. Her voice sounded quavery and out of control. The hammering stopped, and Billy turned, leaning against the wall and looking out at her with unfocused eyes.

"Do you want some sandwiches? I brought you some sandwiches." The words stuck and choked in her throat, but he didn't notice. His blank stare was still aimed in her direction, as if she had waked him up and he was trying to remember who she was.

"Why don't you just leave it?" he said finally, turning back to the wall. "Thanks for bringing it down. I want to get this board done."

He picked up the wrecking bar and began prying another board away from the beams. Julia knelt down on the earth at the edge of the cement cage platform and put the tray of sandwiches and the beer next to the outside of the wrought-iron grille. Her head felt heavy. The floor was cool, and she felt like crumbling from her knees and lying there in the soft dirt. She wondered how long it would take her husband to notice her broken, inert body lying there.

"What's the matter with you now?" he would say. Through the bars she could see his back moving as he pried at the board. The groaning sound as wood separated from wood echoed in her head. As she lifted herself off her knees, she noticed the key protruding from the iron box on the gate of the grille. Stupid Billy, he had locked himself in again. She was about to call to him. If she pointed it out, he would come away from his work and they would laugh together over the mistake. Then she remembered that they didn't laugh over things together anymore. She slipped the key out of its place in the lock and slid it into the pocket of her shorts.

Chapter 16

ACH BOARD LOCKED TO THE ONE below it, resting neatly tongue-in-groove. The rhythm of hammering hypnotized him as if the pounding were an echo of some primitive heartbeat. The new piece of wall, boards mortised together and flat against the beams, had a satisfying professional look. Billy would finish this job and go on to other jobs, keeping his sense of accomplishment bobbing afloat on the warm water of summertime days. The last of the old boards would be off by dinnertime.

A soft visceral hand rubbed the inside of his stomach, and he remembered the beer and sandwiches waiting for him in the hallway. He hadn't wanted to talk when Julia brought

them down. Now that he was enjoying this, she would probably think of something else he should be doing. If he
carried the sandwiches to the wall, he could work and eat at
the same time. He walked over to the bars and turned sideways to step through them, reaching out to push at the gate
of the grille. It was shut. Careless, he had locked himself in
again. His hand reached along the edge of the box for the
key, but it wasn't there. Billy strained his eyes in the dim
light to see if it had fallen onto the cement slab or away in
the dirt. Both surfaces looked smooth and uninterrupted. He
got down on his knees and patted his hands along the cement. Pushing his body against the iron, he reached through
it with his arms and felt along every inch of the dirt floor
within his reach. There was nothing there. He was really
hungry now. By turning sideways, he was able to take the
sandwiches off their tray and lift them through the ironwork.
The beer can had to be passed from one hand to the other and
then angled through a gap in the grille where the ivy twined
into the laurel branches. If he called Julia, she could probably hear him from the house. But then she would come down
and find him and get the key, wherever it was, and let him
out, and he'd never get the rest of those boards off this afternoon.

Mustard and mayonnaise oozed from between the bread
and the ham when he bit into the sandwich. The beer washed
it down, cutting through the chewy aftertaste of the bread
and mixing with the tart Gulden's and the richness of
Hellmann's Whole Egg. Later, when Julia came down to get
him for dinner, she would help him find the key and let him
out. For once he would really need her help. Maybe that
would cheer her up.

He returned to the wall with renewed spirits, but the hammer didn't land with the same accuracy it had before he ate his lunch. Its misses left round, hoof-shaped scars in the wood around the nails. Instead of letting his clumsiness bother him, he put down the hammer and worked with the wrecking bar. The summer was going well. Cece was coming to visit them. This kind of mindless manual work was the best thing for his heart—and for his soul. He began to hum. "Heart and soul, I fell in love with you. Heart and soul—"

Julia's voice surprised him and he jumped, dropping the bar with a clang onto the cement.

"Hi. It's dinnertime," she said. He twisted around quickly. Through the bars she looked surreal again, and her voice sounded as if it was coming from another part of the barn.

"Wait a minute." He picked up the bar and pulled on the last board. It came away from the wall with a shriek. "There, that's the last one." He put the tool down next to the hammer and walked over to the edge of the cage.

"I brought you a drink," she said, handing him a martini through the grille and the bars. It was a big glass.

He took a long swallow of the vodka, letting the ice cubes rest against his upper lip. The strength of the raw alcohol relaxed the muscles in his neck and shoulders. "Thanks," he said.

Julia looked relaxed and attractive. The outline of her high breasts showed through her pale yellow polo shirt. Her long slightly bowed legs glistened smooth and tan below the crisp edge of her khaki shorts. Through the bars she suddenly seemed sensual and desirable.

"You'll never guess," he said. "I seem to have locked myself in again."

"No kidding." Her voice was silky, but there was something wrong under the veneer of friendliness. She kept her head down, and her eyes avoided his.

"I can't find the key. It's not in the lock. Is it out there on the floor somewhere?"

"I don't see it."

"Could you look a little harder? It must be there somewhere."

She bent her head as if to look, and then shook it negatively. "I don't think it's on the floor," she said. "Do you want me to bring your dinner down here?"

He tipped the glass back up against his face, finishing off the drink. Sometimes it took her awhile to understand a situation. He would have to make it clearer.

"Julia," he spoke slowly and deliberately. "I am locked in this cage. What I want you to do is find a way to get me out. I don't think you realize the seriousness of this problem." He was close to her now, staring into her blue eyes through the curves of iron.

She shrugged. "It's not the end of the world," she said.

"What?" Clearly he would have to explain it again, more patiently.

"I said it's not the end of the world. You could stay in there and finish that job you care so much about. There's straw to sleep on. Darwin slept in there a few times."

"Are you crazy?" Inside her eyes he saw something flicker and flip over, like the look in an animal's eyes just before it turns its head away from a human stare.

"Not so *you'd* notice."

"I don't know what you mean." There was something else going on that he couldn't figure out. A dangerous hidden undertow. "What do you mean, not so I'd notice?" His position, trapped in a cage, confronted by the iron bars, gave his voice a pleading, wheedling quality.

"You know what I mean. If you weren't in such a fog all the time . . ." Her body hiccupped softly as if she was about to burst into tears. Instead, she took a deep breath and squared her shoulders. "If you weren't in such a fog all the time, if you paid a little attention to me sometimes . . ." She paused to catch her breath again, but instead of continuing she dropped her head and looked at the ground. In the fading light he couldn't be sure that she was weeping.

"Are you crying?"

She didn't answer. A tremendous weariness descended on him. As usual with her moods, he didn't know what was going on. As usual he was inadequate and he had hurt her in some way that he couldn't even understand. He had tried to communicate with her, and he had failed, as usual. Suddenly he felt an overwhelming desire to sleep. To curl up in silence somewhere far away, and drift off into unconsciousness and out of the horrible tangle of other people's feelings.

"Come on, Julia, don't get upset now." He calculated that his gentleness would release her sobs. "Don't be sad," he said. After she broke down they would be friends again, and she would find a way to get him out of this damn cage and then they could go back up to the house together and sleep. Oh, sleep! Instead of crying, though, she picked up her head as if she was listening to a faraway voice issuing instructions. Stepping closer to him, she leaned her face against the grille. The iron pushed her cheeks inward, her blue eyes glittered with unshed tears, anger brought a rosy flush to the skin over her cheekbones. For a moment he considered reaching through and grabbing her by the collar.

"I'm sorry, Billy, I'm really sorry," she said. Her long

torso seemed to melt toward him through the bars. This was the crucial moment. If he said the right thing now, it would be over. She would give in and help him, and later they would have some dinner.

"Don't be sorry," he said. "You're just a little upset." She was watching him carefully now, taking in every word. He reached out toward her in a sympathetic gesture. "What is it, sweetie? Is it your period or something?" If he asked her, she would know he was friendly and set him free. Instead, she turned her back to him and walked out of the darkness of the building before he had a chance to say another word.

Chapter 17

HE WOKE UP SHIVERING. The cold seemed to radiate down his back and through his cramped legs as if his blood had turned to ice. His head ached, and a sour taste from his stomach filled his mouth. Something was sticking through his clothes and into his skin, scratching unpleasantly. Slowly he began to remember where he was. He stood up and shook the straw away from his shirt, starting up new cramps in his back and thighs. Each movement triggered a dull, thumping pain just behind his eyes. The night cold had permeated everything, his clothes and his underwear were clammy and damp. A faint light from the early morning sky filtered down from the high windows of the building onto the dirt floor. Billy walked over to the bars, hobbling to minimize the weight on his sore legs. Reaching through, he pushed against the door of the grille. The iron rattled against the tumblers in the lock. He shook the door, pushing it rapidly back and forth. The iron rattled some more, and the noise echoed back and forth from the barn's eaves. But the door didn't open.

As his muscles warmed up, he began to feel the layer of dirt, sawdust, and sweat on his skin from yesterday's hammering and prying. He wiped his hands on his trousers and picked up the wrecking bar. Leaning his back against one of the cage bars, he levered the iron spike through the grille, hooking it around the next bar over, and pulled. There was no response. By hooking the wrecking bar around one of the curls of ornamental iron and through a higher gap at the bottom of the medallion with the fanciful portrait of an elephant, he was able to lean his full weight down on the bar. The iron grille didn't give. Next he jammed the tool between one of the bars and a spray of iron laurel leaves and pulled hard, planting his feet firmly on the cement floor and leaning his entire body back with his arms straight forward and his hands around the wrecking bar. For a moment the iron seemed to relent, but then too late he realized that the wrecking bar was slipping off the spray of laurel and flying out to the other side of the cage while he went down flat on his back on the hard floor. Aching and bruised from the fall, he winched himself up to a standing position and limped over to examine the grille. He had succeeded in inflicting a small scratch on the iron surface, but the curves that imprisoned him were unaltered.

Outside he could see the morning mist rising across the high windows above the valleys of birch and maple.

Through the open door he watched the clouds that covered the lake evaporate and the water begin to shine blue in the sunlight. Darwin Gibbs would say that it looked like a scorcher. He had to get out of here today. When Julia came down they would both be calmer than last night. He would get her to cooperate. If she couldn't find the key, she would call the locksmith in town, or she could get Darwin and a couple of the village men to come up and tear the thing apart. Nothing could resist the right tools.

The cool air inside the building was warming up as the heat from the sun began to bake against the walls. His body relaxed in the temperate air. The patterns of iron made shifting dappled shadows on the smooth floor. The quiet soothed him. It was just a matter of time. Julia was sore at him, all right, but she certainly wasn't planning to keep him locked up in a cage! Cece was coming any day now. The crack of the screen door slamming at the house got him up off the straw and halfway to the bars. His ears pricked up at her footfalls coming across the dewy grass. She followed her shadow into the half-light of the hall.

"Breakfast," she said. She bent over to put a basket of muffins and a glass of orange juice on the floor where he could reach them through the grille. "You must be hungry." As she stood, she picked up the empty martini glass and held it in front of her with both hands. He noticed the tense whiteness of her knuckles where she pressed the beveled edge of the glass.

"I'd like to get out of here first," he said. "Could you look for the key again on the floor out there?"

"I'll bring you some lunch later," she said.

"Let's find the key to this door, it must be out there

somewhere," he said. "Could you put down that empty glass and concentrate for a minute?"

"I was just going to take it up to the house and wash it," she said.

He looked straight into her eyes. They had lost the fearful uncertainty of last night. Her body was held stiff and straight, as if she was preparing herself for an attack.

"I want to get out of here." He enunciated every word through clenched teeth. "Don't you understand?"

"You don't have to talk to me that way," she said.

"Oh, Christ! Why do we have to fight when I'm locked in this ridiculous cage? Please, Julia, do me a favor, consider my situation for once."

"I have considered it." There was a finality in her voice now that was both ominous and revealing.

"Do you have the key?"

"Why, of course not." She blushed, and her military stance collapsed. In her eyes he saw fear, hate, alarm, fear and hate one right after the other like the cherries and apples in the slot machines at Reno. He had hit the jackpot.

"You have it!" he said. But although he felt victorious, his discovery seemed to make her more recalcitrant. Instead of breaking down and confessing everything, she just stood there silently. "How can you be so unconcerned?" he asked. "Are you aware that I spent the night in here on the floor like an animal?"

She shrugged. "I guess I'm tired of being concerned about you and your needs and your job."

"Do you think I like having to worry about *you* all the time?"

"Worried about me? You might be worried, but you aren't ever worried enough to listen. Sometimes I think you care more about your job and your secretary than you do about your own family. Men!'' She spat the last word at the floor.

''Don't be asinine. Do you think it's going to help matters if you hiss at me like that?''

Suddenly Julia laughed, a wild jerking laugh that reverberated off the walls with sharp, unnatural-sounding echoes. ''I guess I don't care whether it helps matters or not anymore,'' she said.

''Julia.'' He changed his approach. ''Are you all right?''

''Am I all right? Am I all right!'' Her voice trilled into a strident high register. ''Now you ask if I'm all right. Now, after twenty years of unnoticed servitude, you suddenly ask me if I'm all right. I'm as all right as anyone could be, married to a man who's about as receptive and loving as that cement wall.''

''Listen, Julia, I've been sweating blood in a high-pressure job all these years to support you and your fancy household and your memories of your father. If I failed to listen to the daily litany of your feminine problems, please excuse me.''

''Oh, you're excused.'' His sarcasm had triggered an ugly change of mood. She leaned against the bars now with her face twisted in an angry, mocking leer. Her skin was smooth and rosy; anger seemed to have made her young. She bent one leg slightly outward to keep her balance, and he noticed the contrast of hard and soft as flesh stretched over bone and muscle. The fight had loosened her stiffness, giving her a sexy wanton look that excited him and dulled his rage. He felt helpless. In her eyes he saw the sparkle of power, and it made her look like a stranger. She could keep him there until she wanted to let him go.

"I'll be back with more food." Her shadow vanished through the big doors, and he heard her feet against the dry grass and then the creak of the old boards as she went up the steps into the house. Through the door he could see that it was a beautiful summer day. At the edge of his vision a stand of birches striped a patch of velvety pasture with early shadows. He thought of the meadow and the woods beyond it and the pleasure of stepping on the springy earth of the old logging roads under the pines on a day like today. In the afternoon heat, he could walk through the long grass at the bottom of the hill down to the lake and let the icy water surprise his sweaty skin. It was a nice day for a canoe trip, a good day for an expedition through the woods to the top of the hill, a great day for just lying on the grass and reading and smelling the summery smells.

Instead, he was locked in a cage. Rage built up inside him. He had earned a vacation, God damn it. He had earned it with long nights and endless rewrites and the pressure of surviving in an office of ambitious men. She had robbed him of the vacation he had earned.

"Bitch!" He spat sour mucus out through the bars at the place where she had been standing. If only she would reach inside the bars again, he could hold her and threaten to brain her if she didn't let him out. He could pull her arm through the bars and twist it behind her, forcing her against the sharp iron until she screamed. If he brought the wrecking bar down hard from above, he might break her wrist with one blow. He searched the grille for a long narrow slit perpendicular to the floor where he would have room to bring the iron down hard on top of her head. Her flat skull bones gave way with a pulpy thud as she fell to the dirt floor.

He had often imagined her funeral. At the graveside he

stood looking lean and stricken in a black suit. Everyone was sympathetic. Everyone felt sorry for him. As a grieving widower, he would quit his job and travel. Oh good, they would say, he's found a way to take his mind off his terrible loss. If he fell in love again they would all approve. It wouldn't be infidelity, or adultery, or any of those ugly things. It would be life goes on.

But the relentless curves and sweeps of the grille were as impenetrable as a fine grid of bars. Giuseppe had done his job well. Laying the wrecking bar back on the ground, he paced slowly back and forth from the bars to the wall and back again. How did prisoners pass the time? He could daydream, or draw a calendar on the wall and cross off the days, or cover the cement with his own excrement. The regular rhythm of pacing calmed him. It was really just an ordinary marital spat; the kind of spat that most couples have all the time. He and Julia had never fought, never even raised their voices, that's why this seemed so melodramatic. Their marriage had been a conspiracy of mutual silence, a union of two people who had never said what they wanted or thought, in order to preserve the pleasant surface of their lives. People who live together as they did can never dare more than half-truths. But they weren't crazy. Of course she was going to let him out, now that she had made her point. She would get lonely and want someone to help with the chores. Cece was coming any day now, and they would certainly have to make up before that. And tomorrow was the day for Darwin Gibbs's weekly visit.

His stomach told him it was lunchtime before she appeared again. There was a raw growling in his gut, and his head ached with hunger. His eyes focused on the can of beer and two fat sandwiches she carried as she walked toward him. Her image was cut into jigsaw pieces by the wild curves of iron.

"I made you sandwiches," she said. "Is there anything special you'd like for dinner?" Her voice sounded cringing and stubborn at the same time. She knew he had a perfect right to be angry with her, but she wasn't going to give in.

"Stay and talk a minute," he said.

"Okay." She leaned against the wall with her hands behind her back. Her left leg was cocked at an angle, with her foot rolled up to the toe of her tennis sneaker. This position pushed her breasts forward, and he could see the shadow of two horizontal clavicle bones in the neck of her pale pink blouse. The chill of the air inside the building had hardened her nipples. It looked as if she wasn't wearing a bra.

"Aren't you going to eat lunch with me?"

"I'm going back up to the house."

Under her scrutiny he knelt down on the cement and slid the sandwiches under the few inches of space at the bottom of the grille. The can of beer was harder to get at. He leaned against the iron and reached through to the cool metal cylinder. Using his other hand, he passed the beer can up toward the gap in the frieze of laurel where he had angled his beer can through at lunchtime the day before. Bending his knees to squat, he pushed with one hand outside the grille and pulled with the other one inside, until the can slipped through. Julia watched him without a word.

He sat cross-legged in front of the sandwiches on the floor and pulled the ring off the top of the can, letting out a hiss of air and a puff of foamy fragrance. Tipping his head back, he filled his mouth with the comforting taste. Holding the sandwich with one hand, he took a big bite. The slices of roast beef didn't separate when his teeth bit into them, and he used both hands to keep the whole thing from falling apart as he pulled the meat away from his mouth. Julia shifted her weight from one leg to the other. He took another swallow of beer and thought about the way he had looked on as the animals ate in the Central Park Zoo. Cece loved to get there at feeding time to see the seals jump clear out of the water for the man who threw them slippery silver fish from a bucket, and the hippos in their green pools gorging with yellow molars the long loaves of sliced bread the keepers propelled from cellophane packages, and the big cats mauling juicy steak pieces.

He bit the sandwich again, stuffing it further into his mouth until he could feel the end of the slice of roast beef. Julia stared at him as he chewed and finally swallowed.

"Do you have to look at me like that?"

"I thought you wanted me to stay."

"I hoped we could talk."

"Go right ahead. You seem more interested in eating and drinking," she said. "As usual."

"Julia, I really am interested in talking about your problems. It's just that I'm very busy. My job takes a lot of my time. You know that."

"Oh, that reminds me." She let her hands fall to her sides and faced the door. "Your beloved office called."

He felt sick. "Anything crucial?"

She shrugged. "I told them you were *busy*." She played the word sarcastically off his own use of it. "I said you'd gone camping up at Franconia Notch and wouldn't be back for a few days."

"What did they say?"

"I'm sure Sherry's devastated, but the rest of them don't

seem to need you to carry on, if that's what you're worried about. Walter Sachs seemed to think the change would do you good.''

This intelligence sent a clammy shiver through his chest. He looked up, straining for more clues to her malevolence. The sandwich dropped back onto the floor.

''Have you heard anything from Cece?'' He had been saving the issue of their daughter to use as an emotional wedge. Surely the thought of Cece's arrival would draw Julia toward him. She would certainly want to present a harmonious marriage to Cece.

''We got a letter from her yesterday.''

''When's she coming?'' An unexpected sharp pain cramped his calf, and he brought his hand down to brace it. Through the scrim of iron he locked his eyes to hers and focused all the authority he had. Blank and unyielding and fearless, she looked back at him without expression.

''She's not coming.''

''What? Did you tell her not to come?''

''No, but thanks for your trust. No, I didn't tell my daughter not to come.''

''Why isn't she coming, then?''

''I guess she doesn't want to see us.''

''Come on, Julia!''

''She and Jerry have decided to get married. They're going to Las Vegas for a quickie wedding.''

''Can you show me the letter?''

''You don't believe me even now, do you?''

He shrugged his shoulders, trying to rid them of the weight of this new defeat. ''I do believe you. Well, that's great, I guess. If she's happy.''

''It's not my idea of great,'' Julia said.

Billy felt a long tearing sensation somewhere above his stomach, as if an old rag there had been cut and was being ripped along the warp, leaving a straight, ragged edge. His head dropped and his eyes landed on the remains of the half-eaten roast-beef sandwich. Strands of meat hung away from the torn pieces of bread. The mayonnaise had formed a yellow, congealed surface.

Julia moved away toward the wall again. He couldn't stop her. For a moment he imagined how they might comfort each other over their daughter's defection. But her stiff back as she walked toward the door erased his tenderness. Maybe he should have called out to her. Maybe he should have reached through the bars to try and connect with her one more time. With the preternaturally sharp hearing of an animal, he could pick up her footfalls as she crossed the grass and stepped up onto the porch. There was the creak of boards and a long pause. She must be just standing there, thinking, or waiting for something. Maybe he should call out to her. Then he heard the louder creak of the screen door opening, and the slam of wood on wood as she walked into the house and it shut behind her.

Chapter 18

CLOUDS OF FINE DUST BILLOWED FROM the mattress and wafted toward the window in the sunlight as Julia pulled the dirty sheets around the wooden bedposts. The clean ones from the linen chest were folded in starchy white squares, and they crackled with freshness and the smell of violets as she threw them over the bed, lining up the ironing creases and tucking the edges into perfect hospital corners. She pulled the bedspread up over the sheets and folded it back against the pillows, rearranged against the headboard for a single sleeper.

In the laundry room behind the kitchen, she uncurled the wet sheets and towels from the center pole of the washing machine and dropped them into the wicker basket. Outdoors, she draped the heavy coils of fabric over the clothesline and pulled them along so that each sheet hung off the rope from its midpoint. The drying laundry flapped in the sun as she pushed her way back and forth through the hanging sheets to arrange the rest of them. Each towel was neatly clipped at the corners with wooden clothespins from the cloth sack suspended from the line near the big pine tree. It was a hot day, and the sheets would be dry by dark.

In the kitchen she applied a thin coat of floor wax to the linoleum with a long brush. As one side dried, she buffed it to a polish with a dry mop. The blue and white squares glowed with the borrowed richness of the wax. With an old white rag she dusted the tables in the living room and the desk in her father's study. In the week she had been at Northwood a fine film of pollen and summer dirt had already settled on every wooden surface.

As she worked, neatly accomplishing each household job in order, her arms and legs began to relax. A lightness invaded her veins, as if the shackles of her life had suddenly turned to light twine. Everything was in order. Everything was under control. Some horrible process of deterioration had been stopped. When she passed a mirror, or caught her reflection in a window glass, the shadows and creases in her face didn't bother her. She was an attractive older woman, a woman of a certain age, with the deep lines and creases that inevitably come with childbearing and middle age. No one could be a pretty girl forever.

Her hold on her marriage had been slipping. She knew it before Billy did, because she had always known how hard she had to work to keep him. Billy Bristol had never fallen in love with her, as she let him think. No, she had singled him out and gone after him and gotten him. She had won him away from the others so neatly that he thought it was his own idea.

Once she had passed Marcia Halloran's room in the dormitory at college as she was going down to meet Billy for a dance at the beginning of homecoming weekend, and she saw Marcia sitting there on the edge of her bed weeping, with her thick dark hair across her face. Julia remembered that because she had known that Marcia was crying over Billy. And the slam of her door after Julia passed, dressed in her nifty pink silk, just confirmed it. Marcia had lost. Julia had won.

It had always been a struggle to hold his attention. There was his job, and men friends wanting him to stay in town for a drink, and sports events, and other, younger women. Lots of wives hadn't managed it. But recently her certainty had been slipping away. Cece was gone, she was getting older, his success at work had given him access to another, more exciting world. Security had been easing off, evaporating from under her, lessening as surely as the edge of an island is inexorably lessened by the sea each year in imperceptible degrees.

At midday, after she had taken his lunch down, she called Darwin Gibbs. She was careful not to hurt the old man's feelings by suggesting that he wasn't needed. Instead, she gave the weather as an excuse: It was so beautiful that they were going climbing, she said. Next week was a long way off. For the moment, her time was completely, satisfyingly filled. The floors and windows and bedrooms beckoned to her housekeeping skills. She had already been up to the garden and raked off some of the carnage.

The strawberry beds were all right, and she lovingly

weeded and pruned them. The fence looked intact, but apparently the deer had just jumped over it. When she thought about them trampling her carefully nurtured plants, a black rage rose in her heart. Nature had become a personal enemy. The deer were brutes, fit for the bloody humiliation of having their bodies tied to the fenders of the hunters' big gas-guzzling cars. She hated them, swift destroyers with their heedless sharp hooves and their insatiable appetites. The thought of them vaulting over the garden fence and landing in the neat fertile rows of vegetables made her feel sick.

She wouldn't let that happen again.

Chapter 19

SOMETIMES IT WAS WARM, AND SUNLIGHT beamed down from the windows, and through the iron curves of the grille he could see the wooden texture of the wall on the opposite side of the building. Sometimes it was dark, and he huddled for warmth into the depths of the straw under the blankets she had brought down. He ate without speaking to her, tearing at the food like an animal even if she stood there watching him. Now it was evening after dinner. He could feel every unevenness in the cement through the thin soles of his sneakers. His nose picked up the scents of dishwasher soap and Ajax from the kitchen of the house, and the fragrance of the hay and the forest beyond that. He could hear every car and truck that passed on the road at the bottom of the hill, and the creaking of oars as the last fisherman rowed home across the lake. As he listened, the sound of a bugler playing taps at some distant summer camp wafted to him on the heavy summer night air.

Above him the fabulous wrought-iron grille loomed in the increasing darkness. With a new sharpness, his eyes seemed to take in the whole pattern at once. For three feet at the bottom, laurel boughs curled above a tangle of ivy in symmetrical rows of hooks, each studded with a dozen tear-shaped iron leaves. Each hook grew from an iron branch that extended into another section where the laurel was slightly denser, the hooks smaller, the leaves more abundant. Just above his own height the pattern opened slightly, as each laurel branch melded into a long crescent-shaped base for the ungainly iron figure of the elephant. The whimsical beast was about the size of a man, its trunk and legs and tail enmeshed on all sides with twisting black vines, as if it might once have tried to escape and the plants were reaching out to hold it forever in the same position seven feet off the floor.

Further up, the laurel and ivy continued their climb, ending in a long rail of iron about two feet from the slanted, peaked roof of the building. There was enough space between the top of the grille and the roof for a man to climb over and lower himself down on the other side. Why hadn't he noticed it before? How could he have been so obtuse? Maybe she was right when she said he was always in a fog. But that was over now. He could already feel the coldness of the iron against his hands as he climbed, and he knew in advance the wild exhilaration of his body as he eased himself over the grille at the top and started down the other side. For a moment he imagined himself splayed against the vertical metal, caught by searchlights from a guard tower with his arms and feet spread helplessly apart. He heard the staccato roar of automatic-rifle fire, and felt his torso slump and fall as the bullets splashed his clothing with bloody holes. That was in movies; not in his life.

He took off his shirt and chino pants and folded them in a pile near the edge of the grille along with the hammer and wrecking bar. After he was over he could reach in and get them. If only he had bothered to bring a ladder down! But he could already feel the joy of being on the other side, silently dressing and sneaking out of the building and up the hill past the big balsam and the gardens to the road, while she slept oblivious in her ancestral four-poster. Until now he hadn't dared to think about freedom; suddenly it was dazzlingly, tantalizingly close. Once he got to the road he could hitch-hike. Or walk into Granville Center and take the early bus that came through from North Conway on the way to Boston. By the time she came down with his breakfast he would be making innocent conversation with the man in the next seat as he watched the broad pine woods of Route 93 disappear behind him to the north and every minute brought them closer to the safety of Boston, the anonymity of a big city.

He warmed up for the climb by reaching for the ceiling and then letting his hands drop toward the floor, feeling the stretch in his back and the tingling along the back of his legs. Then he propped one foot in a crook of the laurel and bent over toward it, letting his thigh muscles out as he reached for his toes. Finally he dropped to the ground, keeping his body stiff and raising his weight by pushing upward with the palms of his hands. His arms and shoulders burned. Taking a deep breath he stood up again, pushing his shoulders up and back as he contemplated his assault. The impassive sweeps and circles of iron looked smaller in the darkness. It was nighttime, but his eyes had already adjusted to the change, and each potential toe- and hand-hold was clearly visible. Bending down, he double-tied the laces of his sneakers and hitched up the waist of his boxer shorts.

His right foot rested securely on the first curve of ivy. With his right hand he reached up above the laurel to the crescent-shaped base of the elephant, shifting his weight from the ground to his right foot. His left hand reached for the animal's leg, while his left foot searched for a toehold in the laurel. His toe finally stuck between two of the iron leaves, and he carefully shifted his weight up to that foot. The metal pressed painfully through the top of his canvas shoe as he groped for a handhold further up. There were no horizontals in this part of the design; he wrapped his sweating palm around one of the vertical iron branches above a cluster of leaves and pulled his weight up so that both feet now rested on the base of the elephant. Above him the iron seemed to be denser. The only toehold was as high as he could stretch. He brought his foot up above the animal, doubling over and grazing his face with his knee, and wedged the toe of his sneaker in between two of the leaves. For a moment he looked down between his legs. His pile of clothes and tools on the floor looked small and very far away.

The next reach with his right hand was for the top edge of the frieze of laurel. He strained upward to grab the horizontal iron, but as his fingers closed around it he felt a sharp tearing in the muscles along his back and across the top of his shoulder. His right foot popped out of its precarious hold and swung free in the air. The rubber sole of his left sneaker began to slip along the slant where he had planted it. He tensed his leg muscle to keep his foot still. The rubber let out a squeak as it continued to slide. Clenching his right hand into a desperate fist around the last secure hold, he twisted his head to the right in search of a gap in the iron where his foot would be secure. A spasm of pain shot up the right shoulder and into his hand, loosening his fingers as surely as if an invisible hand were slowly prying them off. He pawed the air with his left hand, bruising his knuckles against the grille. The sound of canvas tearing as his weight wrenched the sneaker out of its hold was the last noise he remembered as he fell.

At first the darkness was so black that he wasn't sure if he had opened his eyes or not. Except that when he closed them again, red and yellow spots swam into his vision. Great weights pinioned his arms and legs to the floor, and his mouth tasted of rust and salt. The effort of moving anything heavier than his eyelids seemed impossible, and he slipped back into unconsciousness. A shift in the light startled him awake again. She would be coming soon.

Knives stabbed into his calves as he lifted himself into a sitting position. There was blood on the palms of both hands, and one knee was split open, with thick scabs forming around the paler pink of a wound. There were scrapes on his thigh, and his right arm was torn below the elbow. The surface of his skin throbbed as he stood upright, each scrape and sore pulling against the edges that had healed while he lay there. No bones were broken. The clothes he had neatly folded before the climb would cover the blood and scabs if he kept his right arm down, and if he was careful not to rub bleeding flesh against fabric.

The waistband of his pants was loose, and the cuffs just grazed the ankle bone. He hitched the belt an extra notch around the shirt. The clothes seemed to belong to a shorter, plumper version of himself. The kind of man who would mount an unprepared attack on a fifteen-foot-high ornamental grille in the middle of the night. Plans clicked through his brain; his past passivity and reticence seemed to have been knocked out of him by the fall. For a moment, lying there, he had forgotten who he was. Now, as his knowledge of himself re-formed, everything seemed slightly different; his perspective had changed. All his experience took on a new significance. He had been waiting around all his life for people to recognize his worth. He had worked hard, and kept his word, and conformed to the unspoken gentleman's code because somehow he had thought that this would be noticed and rewarded. Like Frank Cushing, he had lived as he had been taught to live, and expected the world to value him for it. That was never going to happen.

When he heard the screen door slam and the creak of the boards on the porch and her tread coming across the grass, he arranged his body on the straw in a languorous sprawl that he hoped would suggest the helplessness and powerlessness he knew she anticipated. Inside, his nerves and muscles vibrated with a new power, his cortex hummed with the acuteness of a man who was ready to take his life into his own hands.

"Good morning." She stooped to put the tray of muffins and juice on the floor. Straightening up, she stared at him through the gloom.

"Thanks," he said.

"Is there anything special you'd like for lunch?"

The irony of the question, the strangeness of the jailer

pretending to cater to the prisoner's appetite, seemed terribly funny, but he controlled his reply. "No thanks, Julie."

Something in his voice must have betrayed him. She stepped right up to the grille and pushed her nose through to get a closer look. "Are you okay?" she said.

Under the circumstances, her almost-motherly concern was about the funniest thing he had ever heard. She kept him locked in a cage and then worried about his health? He pressed his hands against his stomach as he lay there, to keep himself from bursting into a great bawdy robust laugh. His voice would be deeper, his breath would come from the bottom of his lungs.

"Darwin Gibbs isn't coming today," she said.

"Oh, why not?"

"He called to tell me he was sick." With unaccustomed certainty he knew she was lying. Her pathetic, mean little face peered down at him, hoping for a reassuring reaction. Darwin Gibbs had been his last hope for help from the outside, and even Julie's limited intelligence had probably figured that one out. With a pleasant little stroke of recognition, he realized that he had always known that help wasn't coming from the outside; he would have to help himself. The urge to laugh again seemed to be pushing up through his legs and into his torso and diaphragm. Julia's lies were so sad, her petty machinations so ridiculous. They had never been able to tell each other the truth. With a heroic effort he repressed his real, authoritative voice and acted out the whiny, mingy tones he knew she expected.

"Gee, sweetie," he said. "I hope you let me out soon." Just beneath the sniveling surface of his voice he could feel a great basso profundo about to erupt in shouts and laughter.

"Well, maybe tomorrow we could go down to the lake,"

she said. If he was tame, it might be all right to let him out for an afternoon airing. Would she want him to wear a leash like an organ-grinder's monkey? This image released a new wave of inner hilarity. Mirth rose in his throat and threatened to choke him.

"That would be nice, sweetie," he said, concentrating on a reedy, wheedling tone.

"Bon appetit," she said. At this final fillip of pretension he was forced to dig his chin into his chest to stifle his reaction. Bon appetit, indeed! When he had listened to her footsteps all the way across the grass and heard the creak of the loose board on the porch and the slam of the screen door, he filled his lungs with air and dropped his shoulders and let his voice out in a deep rolling laugh that filled the high space of the building and rumbled against the walls, striking echoes everywhere. There was no keeping him in this cage anymore. The walls themselves could barely contain his laughter.

The years of captivity fell away from him. He was Nat Turner. He was Emiliano Zapata. He was Steve McQueen tunneling under the barbed wire of the Nazi concentration camp. He was Clint Eastwood swimming across the current away from Alcatraz. Julia's desperate feminine shrewdness would never be a match for a free man. She didn't love him after all; she only wanted to keep him. The weights that had stooped him into passivity—the weight of his job, and her dependence; the weight of his child, and Julia's inability to have more children; the weight of her dwindling trust funds and bitter nostalgia—all rolled off him like a cascade of boulders that suddenly race bouncing down a steep hillside when one small rock beneath the front stone shifts in its place.

Chapter 20

H E WALKED THE LENGTH OF THE cage and back again, the width of the cage and back again, letting the rhythm of his stride obliterate his conscious mind. The solution to his problems was waiting there for him to discover it. Relaxed as an animal, he waited with confident patience. His means of escape would be revealed to him. Scanning the floor after about an hour he suddenly saw it, just as he had known he would, as clearly as if some omniscient power had spoken in stentorian tones from the darkness under the eaves. There was a man-sized hole in the cement floor of the cage. Capped by an ornamental iron cover, it led, he knew, to the subterranean heating and draining system in the cellar under the building. From there he would find access to the outside.

The cover gave a promising shake and crunch when he pried at its edge with the wrecking bar. The concrete around it was old, and crumbled easily. Rusting iron bolts held the cover down, and by chipping around them he was able to uncover the threads of the westernmost one in a few minutes. With a few hours' work he would be able to expose the bolts, pull them out, lift the cover, and slide down into the darkness below. If he worked all night after she had brought him dinner, he could free the iron from the stone well before dawn. During the day he would disguise the loosened iron and gaping holes with piles of straw. Tomorrow night he would lower himself down into the antique heating system and disappear forever.

He had two jobs. One was to pull out the bolts and free the heating cover so that he could get out. The other was to keep Julie from suspecting that anything had changed. It was hard. At dinnertime he was gentle and cringing. All he had to do was behave precisely the way he had been behaving for over twenty years. But it was an almost excruciating effort, more difficult than he could ever have imagined, to project his personality back in time to before his awakening. His life depended on reproducing his own image. After decades of suppression, he had an almost irresistible instinct to cry out, to laugh, to destroy her brittle façade with a few explosive words of truth. He concentrated on controlling his face feature by feature, puffing out the new gauntness of his cheeks and masking the manly steel in his eyes. He tried to press his voice up against his palate and through his nose, to disguise its new resonance. The wolf in Cece's storybook had put chalk in his throat when he spoke, so that Little Red

Riding Hood would think he was her grandmother. He imagined schoolboard chalk rolling under the wild wolf's tongue like a peppermint.

Picking gently with the wrecking bar, he chipped the cement away from the two iron bolts. At first the excitement cost him his appetite, but as the night wore on he brought the sandwiches she had put out for dinner inside the cage and ate them in robust bites, enjoying the texture of the food and savoring the rush of energy. The bolts weren't more than four inches deep. No one had thought about keeping an elephant from escaping through the floor and along the heating ducts. By the time the midnight constellations shone in through the high windows he was finished. The bolts could be lifted neatly out of their enlarged holes with his fingers. He replaced them and covered the debris with straw.

Three times during the day she came down to feed him. Her footsteps on the grass released a pounding inside him, but it wasn't at all like fear. Anxiety sharpened his performance in the once-in-a-lifetime role as the Billy Bristol who had been Julia's well-behaved husband. As he heard her coming, he would begin to think himself into the character, like an actor waiting in the wings for his cue. Slumping down to look shorter he rehearsed the stiffness of his gestures, and the mumbling, half-apologetic tone of the voice that she was used to hearing. He kept a few feet back from the grille so that the iron scrim would blur her vision. He moved back and forth to distract her attention from the loosened bolts and their straw camouflage. At lunch he complained, in the swallowed syllables of his past diffidence, that he was tired of sandwiches. He whined. She brought him lobsters for dinner, and his heart skipped with lust for the strong shell-cracker and picks that lay on the plate. It would be too dangerous to pocket them. He longed for a flashlight, even the uncertain wavering flame of a candle, to illuminate the darkness below the earth in the winding labyrinth of pipes and tunnels.

Eight o'clock. Through the windows he could see the evening star. From the house he could hear the low roar of the dishwasher in its dry cycle. There was no reason for her to come back before breakfast. He pushed aside the straw and pulled the bolts out of the cement and through the iron cover. Bending his knees to take the pressure off his back, he stooped and lifted the edge of the cover, turning it over onto the cement silently and gently. The two empty bolt holes flanked the bottomless darkness of the heating duct. Billy sat at the edge of the hole and counted to ten to control the ecstatic beating inside his chest.

He tucked the hammer in his belt and lowered himself into oblivion. A flat ledge about three feet below the level of the floor stopped him. This was probably where the chimney cut out through the layer of flashing around the furnace itself. Gingerly he rested his weight on the ledge, still clinging with his cut hands to the ragged edge of the floor. If he could get around the chimney and down into the space between the flashing and the furnace, he could hammer his way out. He leaned back against the rough brick sides of the cylinder, and one foot slipped slightly on the flaking surface. The bricks hooked the hammer out of his belt and it fell, making a soft thud on the ledge and then a final clang as it struck a metal bottom somewhere below him in the dark.

Bending his knees, he extended his right leg further down, searching for another ledge or a foothold in the brick. What if he somehow got into the furnace and landed in the great cindery belly of the heating system? What if the furnace door was latched from the outside? To keep his courage he moved quickly, letting his weight rest on a narrow piece of metal protruding from the brick wall. He gripped the ledge with his hands and pushed his left foot against the opposite side of the hole for balance. The rubber sole of his shoe slipped against the grimy surface of the bricks and he sat down hard on the ledge he had been standing on a moment ago. Above him a halo of light came down through the circular opening from the comparative brightness of the cage. He reached down again with the other foot, turning his ankle to find a foothold. There was nothing. Once again he felt fear rising up to meet him from the limitless darkness at the bottom. He braced his hands on the ledge and pushed all his weight evenly against both feet, letting them slip slowly down the surface of the bricks. By keeping steady pressure on the sides of the hole with his hands, he controlled his speed. For a moment, his feet slid evenly and safely down the wall, but then suddenly the bricks ended and the cylinder expanded outward. Billy's feet shot forward into nothingness and his hands flailed helplessly. As he fell, terror, and then a great irrational contentment, possessed his mind. A sharp metal edge tore at his clothes as he tumbled over it. Time seemed to slow down in order to give him a moment to consider his own fate. He considered it, and he accepted it.

He landed, with his eyes still open, a split second later. There was a sharp pain in his right thigh, and his hands were skinned. He held one hand up in front of him, but the darkness was so complete that he had to reach up and touch it with the other hand to be sure it was really there. Pulling himself up to his knees, he cracked his head against a hard surface. He lay back and flexed his muscles. Right arm, right leg, left arm, left leg. If something was badly broken, he would never get out. She would find him helpless and trapped here in the morning. His ribs seemed to be in place. Moving was painful but possible. He crawled forward on bent elbows and knees to avoid the obstacle above him. After a minute the quality of the darkness changed, and he could see that he had fallen out through a break in the flashing and into the cellar. Above him the rusted-out tin made a pattern of great gaping holes. The giant furnace brooded on his right. Below it was a dusty pile of ash and cinders that had been dislodged by his tumbling body.

Pushing his knees forward, he stood up next to the furnace. A few feet off to the left a paler square within the darkness led him to a door. During the fall he had lost his sense of time. Delay would be fatal. He had to be away by morning. He stepped into the larger room. There was more light there, but still no indication of the time, no connection to the real darkness on the outside of the building. Another patch of darkness within the darkness drew him to the north wall. Next to it was a round hole in the wall, with some rusted shreds of metal protruding from its bottom edge at an angle. The wood chute. He remembered the great logging trucks and the men loading wood into the chute from above and Darwin giving orders in the bright autumn sunshine. He would get out through the wood chute. Peering into the hole, he could see that the metal part of the chute, which joined the cellar to the ground above, was completely rusted out. He leaned into the hole and looked upward. There was no change in the quality of the darkness. Nothing was filtering in from the outside. The ground-level entrance to the wood chute had been sealed off.

He stepped backward out into the room again. Next to the useless wood chute, the larger square of darkness on the wall drew his attention. On examination, he saw that it was a sheet of black industrial plastic that had been set into the wall and nailed to the cinder blocks with one-inch strips of molding. Idly, he picked at the molding with his fingers, wondering what the layer of shining plastic might conceal. Then he remembered the bulkhead next to the wood chute on the north side of the building. There in the grass were two iron doors set in the earth at the edge of the wall like ordinary cellar doors. Darwin Gibbs used to sit on them and eat his lunch sometimes.

With his hands he tore off a strip of the molding and plunged it into the soft center of the plastic, releasing a torrent of straw and dust. He breathed deeply and regularly as he worked, slicing the plastic open to the ground and pulling stuffing out of the hole with his hands. Behind it was a flimsy wall of Sheetrock nailed to two-by-fours. Another easy job, but his arms ached and the pulled muscle across his shoulder began to throb. Standing to one side, he pried the edge of the wall away from the beams with his fingers. It gave all of a sudden, caving in toward him, and was followed by a dusty fall of hay, rocks, and dirt. A small boulder bounded out onto the canvas top of his sneakers, bruising his foot. Limping slightly, he cleared the debris away from the first of five concrete steps—the kind of steps that lead up to a bulkhead door from the inside. Suddenly he knew that the door would not be locked. It wouldn't be too late when he got there.

Working with his hands, he cleared a path up the stairs to the inner side of the double doors. A chain and padlock blocked his way, but through the cracks in the iron sheathing he could see outdoors where the nighttime darkness was just beginning to ease off into dawn. It would be about four in the morning. He had plenty of time.

At first, the links in the chain seemed impregnable. They were rusted but secure. When he examined the padlock, it too looked tightly locked. Then he noticed that the padlock wasn't locked to the length of chain that went through the door; an already-locked chain had just been looped through the handles. The corroded iron grated on his skinned palms as he pulled it. He braced his feet against the second stair and pushed against the metal bulkhead with his good shoulder. Slowly, with a great creak, the iron doors gave and opened. Carefully he slipped out between them into the sparkling air and closed them behind him.

As he faced up the hill toward the driveway and the road, a strange lightness seized his body. His blood felt fizzy and sweet. Behind him the lake shimmered like a mysterious jewel at the bottom of the pasture. Mist rose from the valleys to the south. For a minute the silence was absolute, and then he heard the first calls of the morning birds.

Billy stretched his body upward, relishing every soreness because he felt as if he could touch the sky. His lungs filled up with air as if he were breathing for the first time in his life. There was one light on in the kitchen of the house, but above it the brooding turrets and the bedroom windows were silent and safe. Light from the east silhouetted the great balsam tree up the hill where the woods thinned and the driveway led to the border of the property. He brushed the cinders out of his hair and wiped the dirt off his face with the back of his hand. In the west, the reflected dawn began to form pink stripes around the tops of the mountains. The last stars faded. He turned and walked across the meadows toward the road.

Chapter 21

JULIA SAT WITH HER BACK AGAINST the big tree in the edge of the path to the garden. In the autumn there were acorns under the oaks, and in the summer long green maple pods that children could split open and stick on their noses like vertical beaks. Ahead of her, the beehive pattern of the garden fence was coming into focus. It must be almost dawn. This was the time when the deer would come, but this time she would be waiting for them. She remembered how her father and Darwin Gibbs would leave the house before dawn to stalk the marauding animals and be back just in time for breakfast.

She leaned to the right and pushed herself into a standing

position. Now she could see the old swing bolts above her on the branch. She moved with infinite slowness, breathing through her nose to keep a silence that would fool even the animals. A snapped twig, a cough, the crunch of a human shoe in the underbrush, and there would be the white flash of a tail and the end of her chances. In the east, the night moved up out of the sky and the pearly clouds began to be visible at the edge of the horizon, which was the tree-lined ridge at the top of the hill. One minute there was the eerie total silence of a north-country night, and the next minute she heard the manic chirping of the first birdsong. The low and high notes of the bobwhite, and the flickers' crazy chatter, came from the direction of the garden. If the deer were coming, they would come now.

With her utmost stealth, she inched the rifle up to a position against her shoulder. The bullets were already clipped in. Her mother had always been afraid of the guns. There were endless warnings and anxieties about the possibility of someone getting hurt. Over her protests, Julia's father had taught his daughter to shoot. First they had spent summer afternoons together setting up targets. Later he let her come into the woods with him and Darwin when they went to shoot a coon or pop away at the red squirrels.

The light was coming up too quickly. If there was no movement soon, she would have to wait until tomorrow. At least the strawberries would be safe. Julia brought the gun level with her eyes and aimed down the barrel. The metal sight bisected her vision. She lined it up with the path toward the fence and willed the deer to materialize in the path of the bullet. The light was dangerously bright now. An animal could see her if it happened to look toward the big balsam. Suddenly she knew it wasn't going to be tonight. The deer weren't coming. Their time was past. While she waited for them in the dampness with her feet falling asleep in the cold grass, they snuggled secure in their thickets on soft warm mounds of pine needles deep in the forest.

She had relaxed the wooden stock against her shoulder when she heard the first sound. Something was coming toward her up the hill. There was a stealthy but unmistakable footfall below the driveway. With her heart beating wildly, she steadied the gun and squinted down the barrel, shifting it to the left toward the sound. Whatever it was was still not in her line of vision, but she could hear it advancing rapidly. She resisted the temptation to lower the gun and look. Her father had taught her to wait until the target came into the sight line.

The noises were coming closer now. Delicate quick steps with the sure-footed grace of a wild animal. Julia held her breath. It was just west of the driveway now, dancing toward her along the ground, barely disturbing the leaves and grass in its path, so airy, so free was its tread. She tensed her hand against the trigger, squeezing the gun against her shoulder for stability. First a shadow fell against her line of vision, and then a denser mass appeared. A form blotted out the landscape of meadow and trees beyond the sight of the gun. Julia took final, steady aim and began pulling back. The gun responded perfectly, her position was confident and correct, she could almost feel the exact synchronization as hammer hit bullet and powder ignited and the shot flew deadly from the barrel. She fired.

About the Author

SUSAN CHEEVER's first two novels, *Looking for Work* (1980) and *A Handsome Man* (1981), brought the author wide praise and established her as an exciting new talent in American fiction. Born in New York City in 1943, Susan Cheever was graduated from Brown University. She has been a teacher, a reporter for the *Tarrytown Daily News*, a free-lance journalist, and a writer for *Newsweek* magazine. She is the daughter of the late John Cheever.